Charles Churchill

The Works of C. Churchill

Vol. II. Fifth Edition

Charles Churchill

The Works of C. Churchill
Vol. II. Fifth Edition

ISBN/EAN: 9783337002633

Printed in Europe, USA, Canada, Australia, Japan

Cover: Foto ©Andreas Hilbeck / pixelio.de

More available books at **www.hansebooks.com**

THE

W O R K S

O F

C. CHURCHILL.

IN FOUR VOLUMES.

VOL. II.

J. Taylor del. et sculp.

THE FIFTH EDITION.

L O N D O N:
Printed for JOHN CHURCHILL (Executor to the late
C. CHURCHILL); and W. FLEXNEY, HOLBORN.
M DCC LXXIV.

THE

GHOST.

BOOK III.

I T WAS THE HOUR, when *Hufwife Morn,*
   With *Pearl* and *Linen* hangs each thorn ;
When happy Bards, who can regale
Their Mufe with country air and ale,
Ramble afield, to Brooks and Bow'rs,
To pick up *Sentiments* and *Flow'rs* ;
When Dogs and Squires from kennel fly,
And Hogs and Farmers quit their fty ;

When *my Lord* rifes to the Chace,
And brawney Chaplain takes his place.

These Images, or bad or good,
If they are rightly underftood,
Sagacious Readers muft allow,
Proclaim us in the Country now.
For Obfervations moftly rife
From Objects juft before our eyes,
And ev'ry Lord in Critic Wit,
Can tell you where the piece was writ,
Can point out, as he goes along,
(And who fhall dare to fay he's wrong?)
Whether the Warmth (for Bards we know
At prefent, never more than glow)
Was in the Town or Country caught,
By the peculiar turn of thought.

IT WAS THE HOUR—tho' Critics frown,
We now declare ourfelves in Town,
Nor will a moment's paufe allow
For finding when we came, or how.
The Man, who deals in humble Profe,
Tied down by rule and method, goes;

But they who court the vig'rous Mufe,
Their carriage have a right to chufe.
Free as the Air, and unconfin'd,
Swift as the motions of the Mind,
The Poet darts from place to place,
And inftant bounds o'er Time and Space,
Nature (whilft blended fire and fkill
Inflame our paffions to his will)
Smiles at her violated Laws,
And crowns his daring with applaufe.

Should there be ftill fome rigid few,
Who keep *propriety* in view,
Whofe heads turn round, and cannot bear
This whirling paffage thro' the Air,
Free leave have fuch at home to fit,
And write a *Regimen* for Wit;
To clip our pinions let them try,
Not having heart themfelves to fly.

It was the Hour, when Devotees
Breathe *pious curfes* on their knees,
When they with pray'rs the day begin
To fanctify a Night of Sin;

When

When Rogues of Modefty, who roam
Under the veil of Night, fneak home,
That free from all reftraint and awe,
Juft to the windward of the Law,
Lefs modeft Rogues their tricks may play,
And plunder in the face of day.

But hold—whilft thus we play the fool,
In bold contempt of ev'ry rule,
Things of no confequence expreffing,
Defcribing now, and now *digreffing*,
To the difcredit of our fkill,
The main concern is ftanding ftill.

In *Plays* indeed, when ftorms of rage
Tempeftuous in the Soul engage,
Or when the Spirits weak and low,
Are funk in deep diftrefs and woe,
With ftrict Propriety we hear
Description ftealing on the ear,
And put off feeling half an hour
To *thatch a cot*, or *paint a flow'r*;
But in thefe *ferious* works, defign'd
To mend the morals of Mankind,

We

We muſt for ever be difgrac'd
With all the nicer ſons of Taſte,
If once, the Shadow to purſue,
We let the Subſtance out of view.
Our means muſt uniformly tend
In due proportion to their end,
And ev'ry paſſage aptly join
To bring about the *one* defign.
Our Friends themſelves cannot admit
This rambling, wild digreſſive Wit,
No—not thoſe very Friends, who found
Their Credit on the ſelf-ſame ground.

Peace, my good grumbling Sir—for once,
Sunk in the ſolemn, formal Dunce,   -
This Coxcomb ſhall your fears beguile——
We will be dull—that you may ſmile.

Come METHOD, come in all thy pride,
DULLNESS and WHITEHEAD by thy ſide,
DULLNESS and METHOD ſtill are one,
And WHITEHEAD is their darling Son.
Not He whoſe pen, above controul,
Struck terror to the guilty Soul,

Made Folly tremble thro' her ftate,
And Villains blufh at being Great,
Whilft he himfelf, with fteady face,
Difdaining Modefty and Grace,
Could blunder on thro' thick and thin,
Thro' ev'ry mean and fervile fin,
Yet fwear by PHILIP and by PAUL,
He nobly fcorn'd to blufh at all ;
But HE, who in the Laureat Chair,
By Grace, not Merit planted there,
In aukward pomp is feen to fit,
And by his *Patent* proves his Wit ;
For favours of the Great, we know,
Can Wit as well as rank beftow,
And they who, without one pretenfion,
Can get for Fools a place or penfion,
Muft able be fuppos'd of courfe
(If reafon is allow'd due force)
To give fuch qualities and grace,
As may equip them for the place.

But HE—who meafures as he goes,
A mongrel kind of tinkling profe,

And

And is too frugal to dispense,
At once both Poetry and Sense,
Who, from amidst his *slumb'ring* guards,
Deals out a Charge to *Subject Bards,*
Where Couplets after Couplets creep
Propitious to the reign of sleep,
Yet ev'ry word imprints an awe,
And all his dictates pass for law
With BEAUX, who simper all around,
And BELLES, who die in ev'ry found.
For in all things of this relation,
Men mostly judge from *situation,*
Nor in a thousand find we one,
Who really weighs what's said or done.
They deal out Censure, or give Credit,
Merely from him who did or said it.

But HE—who, *happily serene,*
Means nothing, yet would seem to mean;
Who rules and cautions can dispense
With all that humble insolence,
Which Impudence in vain would teach,
And none but modest men can reach;

B 4

Who

Who adds to SENTIMENTS the grace
Of always being out of place,
And *drawls* out MORALS with an air
A Gentleman would blufh to wear ;
Who, on the *chafteft*, *fimpleft* plan,
As *Chafte*, as *fimple* as the Man,
Without or *Charaƈter*, or *Plot*,
NATURE unknown, and ART forgot,
Can, with much racking of the brains,
And ye·rs confum'd in letter'd pains,
A heap of words together lay,
And, fmirking, call the thing a Play ;
Who Champion fworn in Virtue's caufe,
'Gainft Vice his *tiny bodkin* draws,
But to no part of *Prudence* ftranger,
Firft blunts the point for fear of danger.
So Nurfes fage, as Caution works,
When Children firft ufe knives and forks,
For fear of mifchief, it is known,
To others fingers, or their own,
To take the edge off wifely chufe,
Tho' the fame ftroke takes off the ufe.

Thee,

Thee, WHITEHEAD, Thee I now invoke,
Sworn foe to Satyr's gen'rous ftroke,
Which makes unwilling Confcience feel,
And wounds, but only wounds to heal.
Good-natur'd, eafy Creature, mild,
And gentle as a new-born Child,
Thy *heart* would never once admit
E'en *wholefome* rigour to thy Wit;
Thy *head*, if Confcience fhould comply,
Its kind affiftance would deny,
And lend thee neither force, nor art,
To drive it onward to the heart.
O may thy facred pow'r controul
Each fiercer working of my foul,
Damp every fpark of genuine fire,
And languors, like thine own, infpire;
Trite be each Thought, and ev'ry Line
As *Moral*, and as *Dull* as THINE.

Pois'd in mid-air————(it matters not
To afcertain the very fpot,
Nor yet to give you a relation,
How it eluded *Gravitation*————)

Hung

Hung a *Watch-Tow'r*—by VULCAN plann'd
With fuch rare fkill, by JOVE's Command,
That ev'ry word, which whifper'd here
Scarce vibrates to the neighbour ear,
On the ftill bofom of the Air
Is borne, and heard diftinctly there,
The Palace of an ancient Dame,
Whom Men as well as Gods call FAME.

A *prattling Goffip*, on whofe tongue
Proof of perpetual motion hung,
Whofe lungs in ftrength all lungs furpafs,
Like her own Trumpet made of brafs,
Who with an hundred pair of eyes
The vain attacks of fleep defies ;
Who with an hundred pair of wings
News from the fartheft quarters brings,
Sees, hears, and tells, untold before,
All that fhe knows, and ten times more.

Not all the Virtues which we find
Concenter'd in a HUNTER's mind,
Can make her fpare the ranc'rous tale,
If in one point fhe chance to fail ;

                                     Or

Or if, once in a thoufand years,
A perfect Character appears,
Such as of late with joy and pride
My Soul poffes'd, ere ARROW died;
Or fuch as, Envy muft allow,
The World enjoys in H———— now;
This Hag, who aims at all alike,
At Virtues e'en like theirs will ftrike,
And make faults, in the way of trade,
When fhe can't find them ready made.

All things fhe takes in, fmall and great,
Talks of a *Toy-fhop* and a *State*,
Of *Wits* and *Fools*, of *Saints* and *Kings*,
Of *Garters*, *Stars*, and *Leading-Strings*,
Of *Old Lords fumbling for a Clap*,
And *young Ones full of Pray'r and Pap*,
Of *Courts*, of *Morals*, and *Tye-Wigs*,
Of *Bears*, and *Serjeants* dancing jigs,
Of *Grave Profeffors* at the *Bar*
Learning to *thrum* on the *Guittar*,
Whilft Laws are *flubber'd* o'er in hafte,
And *Judgment* facrific'd to TASTE;

Of *Whited Sepulchres*, *Lawn Sleeves*,
And God's *house* made a *den of thieves*;
Of *Fun'ral pomps*, where Clamours hung,
And fix'd difgrace on ev'ry tongue,
Whilft SENSE and ORDER blufh'd to fee
Nobles without HUMANITY;
Of *Coronations*, where each heart,
With honeft raptures, bore a part;
Of *City Feafts*, where ELEGANCE
Was proud her Colours to advance,
And GLUTTONY, uncommon cafe,
Could only get the fecond place;
Of *New rais'd* Pillars in the State,
Who muft be good as being great;
Of *Shoulders*, on which HONOURS fit
Almoft as clumfily as *Wit*;
Of *doughty Knights*, whom *titles* pleafe,
But not the payment of the *Fees*;
Of *Lectures*, whither ev'ry Fool
In *fecond childhood* goes to fchool;
Of *Grey Beards* deaf to Reafon's call,
From *Inn of Court*, or *City Hall*,
Whom youthful Appetites enflave,
With one Foot fairly in the grave,

By help of Crutch, a needful Brother,
Learning of HART to dance with t'other;
Of *Doctors regularly bred*
To fill the manfions of the dead;
Of *Quacks* (for Quacks they muft be ftill
Who fave when FORMS require to kill)
Who life, and health, and vigour give
To HIM, not one would wifh to live;
Of *Artifts* who, with nobleft view,
Difinterefted plans purfue,
For trembling worth the ladder raife,
And mark out the afcent to praife;
Of *Arts* and *Sciences*, where meet
Sublime, Profound, and *all compleat*
A SET (whom at fome fitter time
The MUSE fhall *confecrate* in *Rime)*
Who humble ARTISTS to out-do
A far more *lib'ral* plan purfue,
And let their *well-judg'd* PREMIUMS fall
On thofe who have no worth at all;
Of *Sign Poft Exhibitions,* rais'd
For laughter more than to be prais'd
('Tho' by the way we cannot fee
Why *Praife* and *Laughter* mayn't agree)

Where

Where *genuine* HUMOUR runs to wafte,
And juftly chides our want of Tafte,
Cenfur'd, like other things, tho' good,
Becaufe they are not underftood.

To higher fubjects now SHE foars,
And talks of *Politics* and *Whores*
(If to your nice and chafter ears
That Term *indelicate* appears,
SCRIPTURE *politely* fhall refine,
And melt It into *Concubine)*
In the fame breath fpread BOURBON's *league*
And publifhes the *Grand Intrigue,*
In BRUSSELS or *our own* GAZETTE,
Makes armies fight which never met,
And circulates the Pox or Plague
To LONDON, by the way of HAGUE,
For all the lies which there appear,
Stamp'd with *Authority* come here;
Borrows as freely from the gabble
Of fome rude leader of a rabble,
Or from the *quaint* harangues of thofe
Who lead a Nation by the Nofe,

As

As from thofe *ftorms* which, void of Art,
Burft from our *honeft* PATRIOT's heart,
When ELOQUENCE and VIRTUE (late
Remark'd to live in mutual hate)
Fond of each other's Friendfhip grown,
Claim ev'ry fentence for their own,
And with an equal joy recites
Parade Amours, and *half-pay Fights,*
Perform'd by *Heroes* of *fair Weather,*
Merely by dint of *Lace* and *Feather,*
As thofe rare acts which HONOUR taught
Our daring Sons where GRANBY fought,
Or thofe which, with fuperior fkill,
—— atchiev'd by *ftanding ftill.*

This HAG (the curious if they pleafe
May fearch from earlieft Times to thefe,
And POETS they will always fee,
With *Gods* and *Goddeffes* make free,
Treating them all, except the MUSE,
As fcarcely fit to wipe their fhoes)
Who had beheld, from firft to laft
How our TRIUMVIRATE had pafs'd

Night's

Night's dreadful interval, and heard,
With ſtrict attention, ev'ry word,
Soon as ſhe ſaw return of light,
On ſounding pinions took her flight.

Swift thro' the regions of the ſky,
Above the reach of human eye,
Onward ſhe drove the furious blaſt,
And rapid as a whirlwind paſt
O'er *Countries*, once the ſeats of *Taſte*,
By Time and Ignorance laid waſte ;
O'er lands, where former ages ſaw
Reaſon and *Truth* the only Law,
Where *Arts and Arms*, and *Public Love*
In gen'rous emulation ſtrove,
Where *Kings* were proud of *legal* ſway,
And Subjects *happy* to obey,
Tho' now in ſlav'ry ſunk, and broke
To *Superſtition*'s galling yoke,
Of *Arts*, of *Arms*, no more they tell,
Or *Freedom*, which with *Science* fell.
By Tyrants aw'd, who never find
The paſſage to their people's mind,

To

To whom the joy was never known
Of planting in the heart their throne,
Far from all profpect of relief,
Their hours in fruitlefs pray'rs and grief,
For lofs of bleffings *they* employ,
Which W E *unthankfully* enjoy.

Now is the time (had we the will)
T' amaze the Reader with our fkil!,
To pour out fuch a flood of knowledge
As might fuffice for a whole College,
Whilft with a true Poetic force
We trac'd the Goddefs in her courfe,
Sweetly defcribing, in our flight,
Each *Common* and *Uncommon* Sight,
Making our journal gay and pleafant,
With things long paft, and things now prefent.

Rivers—once N YMPHS—(a *Transformation*
Is mighty pretty in Relation)
From *great Authorities* we know
Will matter for a *Tale* beftow.
To make the Obfervation clear
We give our Friends an inftance here.

The DAY (that never is fórgot)
Was *very fine*, but *very hɔt* ;
The NYMPH (another gen'ral rule)
Enflam'd with heat, laid down to cool ;
Her *Hair* (we no exceptions find)
Wav'd carelefs floating in the wind ;
Her *heaving breafts*, like *Summer feas*,
Seem'd am'rous of the *playful breeze* ;
Should *fond* DESCRIPTION tune our lays
In *choiceft* accents to her praife,
DESCRIPTION we at laft fhould find,
Baffled and weak, would halt behind.
NATURE had form'd her to infpire
In ev'ry bofom foft defire,
Paffions to raife fhe could not feel,
Wounds to inflict fhe would not heal.
A GOD (his name is no great matter,
Perhaps a JOVE, perhaps a SATYR)
Raging with *Luft*, a GODLIKE flame,
By chance, *as ufual*, thither came :
With gloting eyes the Fair one view'd,
Defir'd her firft, and then purfu'd ;
She (for what other can fhe do ?)
Muft fly—or how can He purfue ?

The *Muse* (fo Cuftom hath decreed)
Now proves her Spirit by her fpeed,
Nor muft one *limping* line difgrace
The life and vigour of the Race.
SHE RUNS, AND HE RUNS, 'till at length,
Quite deftitute of Breath and ftrength,
To *Heav'n* (for there we *all* apply
For help, when there's no other nigh)
She offers up her *Virgin* Pray'r,
(Can *Virgins* pray unpitied there?)
And when the God thinks He has caught her,
Slips thro' his hands, and runs to water,
Becomes a *Stream*, in which the POET,
If he has any Wit, may fhew it.

A *City* once for Pow'r renown'd,
Now levell'd even to the ground,
Beyond all doubt is a direction
To introduce fome *fine* reflection.

Ah, woeful me! Ah, woeful Man!
Ah! woeful All, do all we can!
Who can on earthly things depend
From one to t'other moment's end?

HONOUR,

Honour, Wit, Genius, Wealth, and Glory,
Good lack! good lack! are tranfitory,
Nothing is fure and ftable found,
The very *Earth* itfelf turns round.
Monarchs, nay Ministers muft die,
Muft *rot,* muft *ftink—Ah, me! ah, why!*
Cities themfelves in Time decay,
If *Cities* thus—*Ah, well-a-day!*
If *Brick* and *Mortar* have an end,
On what can *Flefh* and *Blood* depend !
Ah woeful me! Ah woeful Man!
Ah woeful All, do All we can!

England (for that's at laft the Scene,
Tho' Worlds on Worlds fhould rife between,
Whither we muft our courfe purfue)
England fhould call into review
Times long fince paft indeed, but not
By Englishmen to be forgot,
Tho' England, *once* fo dear to Fame,
Sinks in Great Britain's *dearer name.*

Here could we mention *Chiefs of old,*
In plain and rugged honour bold,

To

To Virtue kind, to Vice fevere,
Strangers to Bribery and Fear,
Who kept no wretched *Clans* in awe,
Who never broke or *warp'd* the Law ;
Patriots, whom, in her *better* days,
Old Rome might have been proud to raife.
Who fteady to their Country's claim,
Boldly ftood up in *Freedom's* name,
E'en to the teeth of *Tyrant Pride*,
And, when they could no more, THEY DIED.

There *(ftriking contraft)* might we place
A fervile, mean, degen'rate race,
Hirelings, who valued nought but gold,
By the beft Bidder bought and fold,
Truants from Honour's facred Laws,
Betrayers of their Country's caufe,
The Dupes of Party, Tools of Pow'r,
Slaves to the *Minion of an Hour*,
Lacquies, who watch'd a *Favourite's* nod,
And took a *Puppet* for their *God*.

Sincere and honeft in our Rimes,
How might we praife thefe *happier* times !

How might the Mufe exalt her lays,
And wanton in a Monarch's praife !
Tell of a Prince in ENGLAND born,
Whcfe Virtues ENGLAND's crown adorn,
In Youth a pattern unto age,
So Chaftc, fo Pious, and fo Sage,
Who true to all thofe facred bands,
Which private happinefs demands,
Yet never lets them rife above
The ftronger ties of Public Love.

With confcious Pride fee ENGLAND ftand,
Our *holy Charter* in her hand,
She waves it round, and o'er the Ifle
See *Liberty* and *Courage* fmile.
No more fhe mourns her treafures hurl'd
In *Subfidies* to all the world ;
No more by foreign threats difmay'd,
No more deceiv'd with foreign aid,
She deals out Sums to *petty* States,
Whom *Honour* fcorns, and Reafon hates,
But, wifer by Experience grown,
Finds fafety in herfelf alone.

Whilft

Whilst thus, she cries, my children, stand,
An honest, valiant, *native* band,
A train'd MILITIA, brave and free,
True to their KING, and true to ME,
No *foreign* Hirelings shall be known,
Nor need we Hirelings of *our own.*
Under a just and pious reign
The Statesman's sophistry is vain,
Vain is each vile corrupt pretence,
These are my *natural* defence,
Their Faith I know, and they shall prove
The Bulwark of the KING they Love.

These, and a thousand things beside,
Did we consult a Poet's Pride,
Some gay, some serious, might be said,
But ten to one they'd not be read,
Or were they by some curious few,
Not even those would think them true.
For, from the time that JUBAL first
Sweet ditties to the harp rehears'd,
Poets have always been suspected
Of having Truth in Rime neglected,

That *Bard* except, who, from his Youth
Equally fam'd for *Faith* and *Truth*,
By Prudence taught, in *courtly chime*
To *Courtly ears*, brought *Truth in Rime.*

But tho' to Poets we allow,
No matter when acquir'd or how,
From Truth unbounded deviation,
Which cuſtom calls *Imagination*,
Yet can't they be ſuppos'd to lye
One half ſo faſt as FAME can fly.
Therefore (to ſolve this *Gordian* knot,
A point we almoſt had forgot)
To courteous Readers be it known,
That fond of verſe and falſhood grown,   .
Whilſt we in ſweet digreſſion ſung,
FAME check'd her flight, and held her tongue,
And now purſues with double force,
And double ſpeed her deſtin'd courſe,
Nor ſtops, till ſhe the place arrives
Where GENIUS ſtarves, and DULLNESS thrives,
Where Riches Virtue are eſteem'd,
And craft is trueſt Wiſdom deem'd,

                                    Where

Where COMMERCE proudly rears her throne
In State to other Lands unknown,
Where to be cheated, and to cheat,
Strangers from ev'ry quarter meet,
Where CHRISTIANS, JEWS, and TURKS shake hands,
United in *Commercial* bands,
All of one *Faith*, and that, to own
No God but INTEREST alone.

When Gods and Goddesses come down
To look about them here in Town,
(For Change of Air is understood,
By Sons of Physic to be good,
In due proportions now and then
For these same Gods as well as Men)
By Custom rul'd, and not a Poet
So very dull, but he must know it,
In order to remain *incog.*
They always travel in a fog.
For if we Majesty expose
To vulgar eyes, too cheap it grows,
The force is lost, and free from awe,
We spy and censure eve'ry flaw.

But

But well preferv'd from public view,
It always breaks forth frefh and new,
Fierce as the Sun in all his pride,
It fhines, and not a fpot's defcried.

Was JOVE to lay his thunder by,
And with his brethren of the fky
Defcend to earth, and frifk about,
Like chatt'ring N***, from rout to rout,
He would be found, with all his hoft,
A nine days Wonder at the moft.
Would we in trim our Honours wear,
We muft preferve them from the air,
What is familiar, Men neglect,
However worthy of refpect.
Did they not find a certain friend
In *Novelty* to recommend,
(Such we by fad experience find
The wretched folly of mankind)
Venus might unattractive fhine,
And H*** fix no eyes but *mine*.

But FAME, who never car'd a jot
Whether fhe was admir'd or not,

And

And never blufh'd to fhew her face
At any time in any place,
In her own fhape, without difguife,
And vifible to mortal eyes,
On CHANGE, exact at feven o'clock,
Alighted on the *Weather-Cock*,
Which, planted there time out of mind,
To note the changes of the wind,
Might no improper emblem be
Of her own mutability.

Thrice did *She* found her TRUMP (the fame
Which from the firft belong'd to FAME,
An *old ill-favour'd* Inftrument
With which the Goddefs was content,
Tho' under a *politer* race
Bag-pipes might well fupply its place)
And thrice awaken'd by the found,
A gen'ral din prevail'd around,
CONFUSION thro' the City paft,
And FEAR beftrode the dreadful blaft.

Thofe *fragrant Currents*, which we meet
Diftilling foft thro' ev'ry ftreet,

Affrighted

THE GHOST.

Affrighted from the ufual courfe,
Ran *murm'ring* upwards to their fource;
Statues wept tears of blood, as faft
As when a CÆSAR breath'd his laft;
Horfes, which always us'd to go,
A *foot-pace* in my *Lord Mayor's Show*,
Impetuous from their Stable broke,
And ALDERMEN and OXEN fpoke.

Halls felt the force, *Tow'rs* fhook around,
And *Steeples* nodded to the ground,
ST. PAUL himfelf (ftrange fight !) was feen
To bow as humbly as the *Dean*.
The *Manfion-Houfe*, for ever plac'd
A monument of *City Tafte*,
Trembl'd, and feem'd aloud to groan
Thro' all that hideous weight of ftone.

To ftill the found, or ftop her ears,
Remove the caufe or fenfe of fears,
PHYSIC, in *College* feated high,
Would any thing but *Med'cine* try.
No more in PEWT'RERS-HALL was heard
The proper force of ev'ry word,

Thofe

Thofe feats were defolate become,
A haplefs ELOCUTION dumb.
FORM, *City-born*, and *City-bred*,
By ftrict *Decorum* ever led,
Who threefcore years had known the grace
Of *one, dull, ftiff, unvaried* pace ;
TERROR prevailing over PRIDE,
Was feen to take a larger ftride ;
Worn to the bone, and cloath'd in rags,
See AV'RICE clofer hug his bags ;
With her own weight unwieldy grown,
See CREDIT totter on her Throne ;
VIRTUE alone, had She been there,
The mighty found, unmov'd, could bear.

Up from the gorgeous bed, where Fate
Dooms annual Fools to fleep in ftate,
To fleep fo found that not one gleam
Of Fancy can provoke a dream,
Great DULLMAN ftarted at the found,
Gap'd, rubb'd his eyes, and ftar'd around.
Much did he wifh to know, much fear
Whence founds fo horrid ftruck his ear,

So much unlike thofe peaceful notes;
That equal harmony which floats
On the dull wing of City air,
Grave prelude to a feaft or fair;
Much did he inly ruminate
Concerning the decrees of Fate,
Revolving, tho' to little end,
What this fame trumpet might portend.

Could the FRENCH—no—that could not be
Under BUTE's *active* miniftry,
Too watchful to be fo deceiv'd,
Have ftolen hither unperceiv'd?
To NEWFOUNDLAND indeed we know,
Fleets of war unobferv'd may go,
Or, if obferv'd, may be fuppos'd,
At intervals when Reafon doz'd,
No other point in view to bear
But Pleafure, Health, and Change of Air.
But Reafon ne'er could fleep fo found
To let an enemy be found
In our Land's heart, ere it was known
They had departed from their own.

Or could his *Succeſſor* (Ambition
Is ever haunted with fuſpicion)
His daring *Succeſſor elect*,
All Cuſtoms, rules, and forms reject,
And aim, regardleſs of the crime,
To ſeize the chair before his time ;

Or (deeming this the lucky hour,
Seeing his *Countrymen* in pow'r,
Thoſe Countrymen, who, from the firſt,
In tumults and *Rebellion* nurs'd,
Howe'er they wear the maſk of art,
Still love a STUART *in their heart)*
Could SCOTTISH CHARLES ——

Conjecture thus,

That mental IGNIS FATUUS,
Led his poor brains a weary dance
From FRANCE to ENGLAND, hence to FRANCE,
'Till INFORMATION (in the ſhape
Of Chaplain learned, good SIR CRAPE,
A lazy, lounging, pamper'd Prieſt,
Well known at ev'ry City feaſt,

For

For he was feen much oft'ner there

Than in the Houfe of God at Pray'r ;

Who always ready in his place,

Ne'er let God's creatures wait for grace,

Tho', as the beft Hiftorians write,

Lefs fam'd for Faith than Appetite,

His difpofition to reveal,

The Grace was fhort, and long the meal ;

Who always would excefs admit,

If *Haunch* or *Turtle* came with it,

And ne'er engag'd in the defence

Of felf-denying Abftinence,

When he could fortunately meet

With any thing he lik'd to eat ;

Who knew that Wine, on Scripture plan,

Was made to chear the heart of Man,

Knew too, by long experience taught,

That Chearfulnefs was kill'd by thought,

And from thofe premifes collected,

(Which few perhaps would have fufpected)

That none, who with due fhare of fenfe

Obferv'd the ways of Providence,

Could with fafe Confcience leave off drinking,

'Till they had loft the pow'r of thinking ;

With

With eyes half-clos'd came *waddling* in,
And, having ftrok'd his double *chin*,
(That *Chin*, whofe credit to mainta'n
Againft the Scoffs of the profane,
Had coft him more than ever State
Paid for a *poor Electorate*,
Which after all the coft and rout
It had been better much without)
Briefly (for *Breakfaft*, you muft know,
Was waiting all the while below)
Related, bowing to the ground,
The caufe of that uncommon found,
Related too, that at the door,
POMPOSO, PLAUSIBLE, and M—E,
Begg'd that FAME might not be allow'd,
Their fhame to publifh to the crowd;
That fome new laws he would provide,
(If Old could not be mifapplied,
With as much eafe and fafety there,
As they are mifapplied *elfewhere*)
By which it might be conftrued treafon
In Man to exercife his reafon,
Which might *ingenioufly* devife
One punifhment for Truth and Lies,

And fairly prove, when they had done,
That Truth and Falſhood were but one ;
Which Juries muſt indeed retain,
But their effect ſhould render vain,
Making all real pow'r to reſt
In *one corrupted rotten breaſt*,
By whoſe *falſe gloſs* the very Bible
Might be interpreted a *Libel*.

M****, (who, his Reverence to ſave,
Pleaded the Fool to ſcreen the Knave,
Tho' all, who witneſs'd on his part,
Swore for his *head* againſt his *heart)*
Had taken down, from firſt to laſt,
A juſt account of all that paſt ;
But, ſince the gracious will of *Fate*,
Who mark'd the child for wealth and ſtate
E'en in the Cradle, had decreed
The *mighty* Dullman ne'er ſhould read,
That office of *diſgrace* to bear
'The *ſmooth-lip'd* Plausible was there.
From H***** e'en to Clerkenwell
Who knows not *ſmooth-lip'd* Plausible ?

A

A Preacher deem'd of greateſt note,
For Preaching that which others wrote.

   Had DULLMAN now (and Fools we ſee
Seldom want Curioſity) ·
Conſented (but the *mourning ſhade*,
Of GASCOYNE haſt'ned to his aid,
And in his hand, what could he more ?
Triumphant CANNING's Picture bore)
That *our three Heroes* ſhould advance
And read their *Comical Romance*,
How rich a feaſt, what royal fare
We for our Readers might prepare !
So rich, and yet ſo ſafe a feaſt,
That no *one foreign blatant* beaſt,
Within the purlieus of the *Law*,
Should dare thereon to lay his paw,
And, *growling*, cry, with ſurly tone,
Keep off——*this feaſt is all my own.*

   Bending to earth the downcaſt eye,
Or planting it againſt the ſky,
As *One* immers'd in deepeſt Thought,
Or with ſome holy Viſion caught,

His

His Hands, to aid the traitor's art,
Devoutly folded o'er his heart.
Here M****, in fraud well ſkill'd, ſhould go
All Saint, with ſolemn ſtep and ſlow.
O that RELIGION's ſacred name,
Meant to inſpire the pureſt flame,
A Proſtitute ſhould ever be
To that *Arch fiend* HYPOCRISY,
Where we find ev'ry other vice
Crown'd with *damn'd ſneaking Cowardice !*
Bold Sin reclaim'd is often ſeen;
Paſt hope that Man, who dares be mean.

There, full of *fleſh*, and full of *Grace*,
With that *fine round unmeaning face*,
Which NATURE gives to ſons of earth,
Whom ſhe deſigns for eaſe and mirth,
Should the *prim* PLAUSIBLE be ſeen,
Obſerve his ſtiff affected mien ;
'Gainſt NATURE, arm'd by GRAVITY,
His Features too in buckle ſee ;
See with what Sanctity he reads,
With what Devotion tells his beads !

Now

Now Prophet, fhew me, by thine art,
What's the Religion of his heart ;
Shew *there*, if Truth thou can'ft unfold,
Religion center'd all in Gold,
Shew *Him*, nor fear Correction's rod,
As falfe to *Friendfhip*, as to GOD.

    Horrid, *unweildy*, *without Form*,
Savage, as OCEAN in a Storm,
Of fize prodigious, in the rear,
That Poft of Honour, fhould appear
POMPOSO; *Fame* around fhould tell
How he a flave to int'reft fell,
How, for *Integrity* renown'd,
Which Bookfellers have often found,
He for *Subfcribers* baits his hook,
And takes their cafh—but where's the Book ?
No matter where—*Wife* Fear, we know,
Forbids the robbing of a Foe ;
But what, to ferve our private ends,
Forbids the cheating of our friends ?
No Man alive, who would not fwear
All's *fafe*, and therefore *honeft* there.

For, fpite of all the learned fay,
If we to Truth attention pay,
The word *Difhonefty* is meant
For nothing elfe but *Punifhment.*
Fame too fhould tell, nor heed the threat
Of Rogues, who Brother Rogues abet,
Nor tremble at the terrors hung
Aloft, *to make her hold her tongue,*
How to all Principles untrue,
Not fix'd to *old* Friends, nor to *New,*
He damns the *Penfion* which he takes,
And loves the STUART he forfakes.
NATURE (who juftly regular
Is very feldom known to err,
But now and then in *fportive mood,*
As fome *rude* wits have underftood,
Or *through much work requir'd in hafte,*
Is with a random ftroke difgrac'd)
POMPOSO form'd on *doubtful* plan,
Not quite a *Beaft,* nor quite a *Man,*
Like—*God knows what*—for never yet
Could the moft fubtle human Wit
Find out a Monfter, which might be
The Shadow of a *Simile.*

THESE

THESE THREE, THESE GREAT, THESE MIGHTY

Nor can the *Poet*'s Truth agree,   [THREE,

Howe'er Report hath done him wrong,

And warp'd the purpose of his song,

Amongst the refuse of their Race,

The Sons of Infamy to place,

That open, gen'rous, manly mind,

Which we with joy in ALDRICH find.

THESE THREE, who now are *faintly* shewn,

Just sketch'd, and scarcely to be known,

If DULLMAN their Request had heard,

In stronger Colours had appear'd,

And Friends, tho' partial, at first view,

Shudd'ring, had own'd the picture true.

But had their Journal been display'd,

And the whole process open laid,

What a vast unexhausted field

For Mirth, must such a Journal yield !

In her own anger strongly charm'd,

'Gainst hope, 'gainst Fear by Conscience arm'd,

Then had bold SATIRE made her way,

Knights, *Lords*, and *Dukes*, her destin'd prey.

But Prudence, ever facred name
To thofe who feel not VIRTUE's flame,
Or only feel it at the beft
As the dull dupe of *Intereft*,
Whifper'd aloud (for this we find
A Cuftom current with Mankind,
So loud to Whifper, that each word
May all around be plainly heard,
And Prudence fure would never mifs
A Cuftom fo contriv'd as this
Her Candour to fecure; yet aim,
Sure Death againft another's fame)
Knights, *Lords*, and *Dukes*—mad wretch, forbear,
Dangers unthought of ambufh there ;
Confine thy rage to weaker flaves,
Laugh at *fmall Fools*, and lafh *fmall Knaves*,
But never, *helplefs*, *mean*, and *poor*,
Rufh on, where Laws cannot fecure,
Nor think thyfelf, miftaken Youth,
Secure in Principles of *Truth* ;
Truth! why, fhall ev'ry wretch of Letters
Dare to fpeak *Truth* againft his *Betters !*
Let *ragged* VIRTUE ftand aloof,
Nor mutter accents of reproof;

Let

Let *ragged* WIT a Mute become,
When Wealth and Pow'r would have her dumb.
For who the Devil doth not know,
That Titles and Eftates beftow
An ample ftock, where'er they fall,
Of Graces which we mental call?
Beggars, in ev'ry age and nation,
Are Rogues and Fools by Situation;
The Rich and Great are underftood
To be of Courfe both wife and good.
Confult then Int'reft more than Pride,
Difcreetly take the ftronger fide,
Defert in Time the fimple few,
Who *Virtue*'s barren path purfue,
Adopt my maxims———follow Me———
To BAAL bow the prudent knee;
Deny thy God, betray thy Friend,
At BAAL's altars hourly bend,
So fhalt Thou rich and great be feen;
To be Great *now*, You muft be mean.

Hence, *Tempter*, to fome weaker Soul,
Which Fear and Intereft controul;

Vainly

Vainly thy precepts are addref's'd,
Where VIRTUE fteels the fteady breaft.
Thro' Meannefs wade to boafted pow'r,
Through Guilt repeated ev'ry hour ;
What is thy Gain, when all is done,
What mighty laurels haft Thou won ?
Dull Crowds, to whom the heart's unknown,
Praife Thee for Virtues not thy own ;
But will, at once Man's fcourge and friend,
Impartial CONSCIENCE too commend ?
From her Reproaches can'ft thou fly ?
Can'ft Thou with worlds her filence buy ?
Believe it not—her ftings fhall find
A Paffage to thy *Coward* Mind.
There fhall fhe fix her fharpeft dart,
There fhew Thee truly, *as Thou art,*
Unknown to thofe, by whom Thou'rt priz'd;
Known to thyfelf to be defpis'd.

The Man, who weds the facred MUSE,
Difdains all mercenary views,
'And He, who VIRTUE's throne would rear,
Laughs at the Phantoms rais'd by Fear.

                                        Tho'

Tho' *Folly*, rob'd in Purple, fhines,
Tho' *Vice* exhaufts *Peruvian* mines,
Yet fhall they tremble, and turn pale,
When SATIRE wields her mighty Flail;
Or fhould They, of rebuke afraid,
With MELCOMBE feek Hell's deepeft fhade,
SATIRE, ftill mindful of her aim,
Shall bring the Cowards back to Shame.

Hated by many, lov'd by few,
Above each little private view,
Honeft, tho' poor, (and who fhall dare
To difappoint my boafting there?)
Hardy and refolute, tho' weak,
The dictates of my heart to fpeak,
Willing I bend at SATIRE's Throne;
What Pow'r I have, be all her own.

Nor fhall yon *Lawyer*'s fpecious art,
Confcious of a corrupted heart,
Create imaginary Fear
To damp us in our bold Career.
Why fhould we Fear; and what? the Laws?
They all are arm'd in VIRTUE's caufe.

And

And aiming at the felf-fame end,
SATIRE is always VIRTUE's Friend,
Nor fhall that Mufe, whofe honeft rage,
In a corrupt degen'rate age,
(When, dead to ev'ry nicer fenfe,
Deep funk in Vice and Indolence,
The SPIRIT of old ROME was broke
Beneath the *Tyrant Fidler*'s yoke)
Banifh'd the Rofe from Nero's cheek ;
Under a BRUNSWICK fear to fpeak.

Draw'n by *Conceit* from REASON's plan,
How vain is that *poor Creature,* MAN !
How pleas'd is ev'ry paultry elf
To prate about that thing himfelf !
After my Promife made in Rime,
And meant in earneft at that time,
To jog, according to the Mode,
In one dull pace, in one dull road,
What but that Curfe of Heart and Head
To this *digreffion* could have led,
Where plung'd, in vain I look about,
And can't ftay in, nor well get out.

Could

Could I, whilft *Humour* held the Quill,
Could I *digrefs* with half that fkill,
Could I with half that fkill return,
Which we fo much admire in STERNE,
Where each *Digreffion*, feeming vain,
And only fit to entertain,
Is found, on better recollection,
To have a juft and nice Connection,
To help the whole with wond'rous art,
Whence it feems idly to depart ;
Then fhould our readers ne'er accufe
Thefe wild excurfions of the Mufe,
Ne'er backward turn dull Pages o'er
To recollect what went before ;
Deeply imprefs'd, and ever new,
Each Image paft fhould ftart to view,
And We to DULLMAN now come in,
As if we ne'er had abfent been.

Have you not feen, when danger's near,
The coward cheek turn *white* with fear ?
Have you not feen, when danger's fled,
The felf-fame cheek with joy turn *red?*

Thefe

THE GHOST.

Thefe are *low* fymptoms which we find
Fit only for a vulgar mind,
Where honeft features, void of art,
Betray the feelings of the heart;
Our Dullman with a face was blefs'd
Where no one paffion was exprefs'd,
His eye, in a *fine ftupor* caught,
Imply'd a plenteous lack of thought:
Nor was one line that whole face feen in,
Which could be juftly charg'd with meaning.

To Avarice by *birth* ally'd,
Debauch'd by *Marriage* into *Pride*,
In age grown fond of youthful fports,
Of Pomps, of Vanities, and Courts,
And by fuccefs too mighty made,
To love his Country or his Trade,
Stiff in opinion (no rare cafe
With Blockheads in, or out of Place)
Too weak, and infolent of Soul,
To fuffer Reafon's juft controul,
But bending, of his own accord,
To that *trim tranfient toy*, My Lord;

The

The dupe of SCOTS (a fatal race,
Whom GOD in *wrath* contriv'd to place,
To fcourge our crimes, and gall our pride,
A conftant thorn in ENGLAND's fide,
Whom firft, our greatnefs to oppofe,
He in his vengeance mark'd for *foes* ;
Then, more to ferve his wrathful ends,
And *more to curfe us*, mark'd for *Friends*).
Deep in the ftate, if we give credit
To *Him*, for no one elfe e'er faid it,
Sworn friend of great Ones not a few,
Tho' he their Titles only knew,
And thofe (which envious of his breeding
Book-worms have charg'd to want of reading)
Merely to fhew himfelf polite
He never would pronounce aright ;
An *Orator* with whom a hoft
Of thofe which ROME and ATHENS boaft,
In all their Pride might not contend,
Who, with no Pow'rs to recommend,
Whilft JACKEY HUME, and BILLY WHITEHEAD,
And DICKEY GLOVER fat delighted,
Could fpeak whole days in Nature's fpite,
Juft as thofe *able Verfe-men* write,

        Great

Great DULLMAN from his bed arofe—
Thrice did he fpit—thrice wip'd his nofe—
Thrice ftrove to fmile—thrice ftrove to frown—
And thrice look'd up—and thrice look'd down—
Then Silence broke—CRAPE, who am I?
CRAPE bow'd, and fmil'd an arch reply,
Am I not CRAPE? I am, you know,
Above all thofe who are below.
Have I not knowledge? and for *Wit*,
Money will always purchafe it,
Nor, if it needful fhould be found,
Will I grudge ten, or twenty Pound,
For which the whole ftock may be bought
Of *fcoundrel wits* not worth a Groat.
But left I fhould proceed too far,
I'll feel my Friend *the Minifter*,
(Great Men, CRAPE, muft not be neglected)
How he in this point is affected,
For, as I ftand a magiftrate,
To ferve him firft, and next the State,
Perhaps he may not think it fit
To let *his* magiftrates have wit.

Boaft

Boaſt I not, at this very hour,
Thoſe large effects which troop with pow'r?
Am I not mighty in the land?
Do not I ſit, whilſt others ſtand?
Am I not with rich garments grac'd,
In ſeat of honour always plac'd?
And do not *Cits* of chief degree,
Tho' proud to others, bend to me?

Have I not, as a JUSTICE ought,
The laws ſuch wholeſome rigour taught,
That *Fornication*, in diſgrace,
Is now afraid to ſhew her face,
And not one Whore theſe walls approaches
Unleſs they ride in our own coaches?
And ſhall *this* FAME, an *old poor* Strumpet,
Without our Licence found her Trumpet,
And, envious of our City's quiet,
In broad Day-light blow up a Riot?
If inſolence like this we bear,
Where is our State? our office where?
Farewell all honours of our reign,
Farewell the *Neck ennobling* CHAIN,

Freedom's *known* badge o'er all the globe,
Farewell the *solemn-spreading* ROBE,
Farewell the SWORD,—*farewell* the MACE,
Farewell all TITLE, POMP, and PLACE.
Remov'd from Men of high degree,
(A lofs to *them*, CRAPE, not to *Me*)
Banifh'd to CHIPPENHAM, or to FROME,
DULLMAN once more fhall ply the Loom.

CRAPE, lifting up his hands and eyes,
DULLMAN—the *Loom*—at CHIPPENHAM—cries,
If there be Pow'rs which greatnefs love,
Which *rule below*, but *dwell above*,
Thofe Pow'rs united all fhall join
To contradict the rafh defign.

Sooner fhall ftubborn WILL lay down
His oppofition with his *Gown*,
Sooner fhall TEMPLE leave the road
Which leads to VIRTUE's *mean* abode,
Sooner fhall SCOTS this Country quit,
And ENGLAND's Foes be Friends to PITT,
Than DULLMAN, from his grandeur thrown,
Shall wander out-caft, and unknown.

Sure

Sure as that *Cane* (a *Cane* there ftood
Near to a *Table*, made of *Wood*,
Of *dry fine* Wood a table made,
By fome rare artift in the trade;
Who had enjoy'd immortal praife
If he had liv'd in HOMER's days.)
Sure as that *Cane*, which once was feen
In pride of life all frefh and green,
The banks of INDUS to adorn;
Then, of its leafy honours fhorn,
According to exacteft rule,
Was fafhion'd by the workman's tool,
And which at prefent we behold
Curioufly polifh'd, crown'd with *gold*,
With gold *well-wrought*; fure as that *Cane*,
Shall never on its native plain
Strike root afrefh, fhall never more
Flourifh in Tawny INDIA's fhore,
So fure fhall DULLMAN and his race
To lateft times this ftation grace.

DULLMAN, who all this while had kept
His eye-lids clos'd as if He flept,

Now

Now looking fteadfaftly on CRAPE,
As at fome God in human fhape—
CRAPE, I proteft, you feem to me
To have difcharg'd a Prophecy;
Yes—from the firft it doth appear
Planted by FATE, the DULLMANS *here*
Have always held a quiet reign,
And *here* fhall to the laft remain.

CRAPE, they're all wrong about this *Ghoft*—
Quite on the wrong fide of the Poft—
Blockheads to take *it* in their head
To be a meffage from the dead,
For that by *Miffion* they defign,
A word not half fo good as mine.
CRAPE—*here* it is—ftart not one doubt—
A *Plot*—a *Plot*—I've found it out.

O God!—cries CRAPE,—how bleft the nation,
Where one Son boafts fuch penetration!

CRAPE, I've not time to tell you now
When I difcover'd this, or *how*;

To

To STENTOR go—if he's not there,
His place let *Bully* NORTON bear—
Our Citizens to Council to call—
Let *All* meet—'tis the caufe of *All*.
Let the three Witneffes attend
With *Allegations* to befriend,
To fwear juft fo much, and no more,
As We inftruct them in before.

    Stay—CRAPE—come back—what, don't you fee
Th' effects of this difcovery ?
DULLMAN all care and toil endures—
The Profit, CRAPE, will all be *Yours*.
A *Mitre* (for, this arduous tafk
Perform'd, they'll grant whate'er I afk)
A *Mitre* (and perhaps the beft)
Shall thro' my Intereft make thee bleft.
And at this time, when *gracious* FATE
Dooms to the *Scot* the reigns of State,
Who is more fit (and for your ufe
We could fome inftances produce)
Of ENGLAND's *Church* to be the *Head*,
Than You, a *Prefbyterian* bred ?

                E 3   But

But when thus mighty you are made,
Unlike the Brethren of thy trade,
Be grateful, CRAPE, and let Me not,
Like *Old* NEWCASTLE, be forgot.

But an Affair, CRAPE, of this size
Will afk from Conduct vaft fupplies;
It muft not, as the Vulgar fay,
Be done in *Hugger Mugger* way.
Traitors indeed (and that's difcreet)
Who hatch the Plot, in private meet;
They fhould in Public go, no doubt,
Whofe bufinefs is to find it out.

To-morrow—if the day appear
Likely to turn out fair and clear—
Proclaim a *Grand Proceffionade*—
Be all the City Pomp difplay'd,
Let the *Train-bands*—CRAPE fhook his head—
They heard the Trumpet and were fled—
Well—cries the Knight—if that's the cafe,
My Servants fhall fupply their place—
My Servants—*mine alone*—no more
Than what *my* Servants did before—

                                     Doft

Doſt not remember, CRAPE, that day,
When, DULLMAN's grandeur to diſplay,
As all too ſimple, and too low,
Our City Friends were thruſt below,
Whilſt, as more worthy of our Love,
Courtiers were entertain'd above ?
Tell me, who waited then ? and how ?
My Servants—*mine*—and why not now ?
In haſte then, CRAPE, to STENTOR go—
But ſend up HART who waits below,
With him, 'till You return again
(Reach me my *Spectacles* and *Cane*)
I'll make a proof how I advance in
My new accompliſhment of *dancing*.

Not quite ſo faſt as Lightning flies,
Wing'd with *red* anger, thro' the ſkies ;
Not quite ſo faſt as, ſent by JOVE,
IRIS deſcends on wings of Love ;
Not quite ſo faſt as TERROR rides
When He the chafing winds beſtrides ;
CRAPE Hobbled—but his mind was good—
Cou'd he go faſter than He cou'd ?

Near

Near to that *Tow'r*, which, as we're told,
The mighty JULIUS rais'd of old,
Where to the block by Juſtice led,
The *Rebel* SCOT hath often bled,
Where Arms are kept ſo clean, ſo bright,
'Twere Sin they ſhould be ſoil'd in fight,
Where Brutes of *foreign* race are ſhewn
By Brutes much greater of *our own*,
Faſt by the crouded *Thames*, is found
An ample ſquare of ſacred ground,
Where artleſs *Eloquence* preſides,
And *Nature* ev'ry ſentence guides.

Here *Female Parliaments* debate
About Religion, Trade, and State,
Here ev'ry NAIAD's Patriot ſoul,
Diſdaining *Foreign* baſe controul,
Deſpiſing *French*, deſpiſing *Erſe*,
Pours forth the *plain Old Engliſh* Curſe,
And bears aloft, with terrors hung,
The Honours of the *Vulgar Tongue.*

Here STENTOR, always heard with awe,
In thund'ring accents deals out Law.

Twelve

Twelve Furlongs off each dreadful word
Was plainly and diftinctly heard,
And ev'ry neighbour hill around
Return'd and fwell'd the mighty found.
The loudeft Virgin of the ftream,
Compar'd with *him*, would filent feem ;
THAMES (who, enrag'd to find his courfe
Oppos'd, rolls down with double force,
Againft the Bridge indignant roars,
And lafhes the refounding fhores)
Compar'd with *him*, at loweft Tide,
In fofteft whifpers feems to glide.

Hither directed by the noife,
Swell'd with the hope of future joys,
Thro' too much zeal and hafte made lame,
The *Rev'rend* flave of DULLMAN came.

STENTOR—with fuch a ferious air,
With fuch a face of *folemn* care,
As might import him to contain
A Nation's welfare in his brain—
STENTOR—cries CRAPE—I'm hither fent
On bufinefs of moft high intent,

Great

THE GHOST.

Great DULLMAN's orders to convey;
DULLMAN commands, and I obey.
Big with thofe throes which Patriots feel,
And lab'ring for the common weal,
Some fecret which forbids him reft,
Tumbles and *Toffes* in his breaft,
Tumb.es and *Toffes* to get free;
And thus the Chief commands by Me.

To-morrow if the Day appear
Likely to turn out fair and clear—
Proclaim a *Grand Proceffionade*—
Be all the City Pomp difplay'd—
Our Citizens to Council call—
Let *All* meet—'tis the Caufe of *All*,

END OF THE THIRD BOOK.

THE

GHOST.

BOOK IV.

*C*OXCOMBS, who vainly make pretence
　　To fomething of exalted fenfe
'Bove other men, and, *gravely wife*,
Affect thofe pleafures to defpife,
Which, merely to the eye confin'd,
Bring no improvement to the mind,
Rail at all pomp ; They would not go
For millions to a *Puppet-Show,*

Nor

Nor can forgive the mighty crime
Of countenancing *Pantomime* ;
No, not at COVENT-GARDEN, where,
Without a head for play or play'r,
Or, could a head be found moft fit,
Without one play'r to fecond it,
They muft, obeying *Folly's* call,
Thrive by mere fhew, or not at all.

    With thefe *grave* Fops, who (blefs their brains,
Moft cruel to themfelves, take pains
For wretchednefs, and would be thought
Much wifer than a wife man ought
For his own happinefs to be,
Who, what they hear, and what they fee,
And what they fmell, and tafte, and feel,
Diftruft, till REASON fets her feal,
And, by long trains of confequences
Enfur'd, gives Sanction to the *Senfes* ;
Who would not, Heav'n forbid it! wafte
One hour in what the World calls Tafte,
Nor fondly deign to laugh or cry
Unlefs they know fome reafon why ;

                       With

With thefe *grave* Fops, whofe fyftem feems
To give up Certainty for dreams,
The *Eye* of Man is underftood
As for no other purpofe good
Than as a door, thro' which of courfe
Their paffage crouding objects force,
A downright Ufher, to admit
New-Comers to the Court of *Wit*.
(Good GRAVITY, forbear thy fpleen
When I fay *Wit*, I *Wifdom* mean.)
Where (fuch the practice of the Court,
Which legal Precedents fupport)
Not one Idea is allow'd
To pafs unqueftion'd in the crowd,
But e're It can obtain the grace
Of holding in the brain a place,
Before the Chief in Congregation
Muft ftand a *ftrict Examination*.

Not fuch as *Thofe*, who PHYSIC twirl,
Full fraught with death, from ev'ry curl,
Who prove, with all becoming State,
Their voice to be the voice of Fate,

Prepar'd

THE GHOST.

Prepar'd with *Effence*, *Drop*, and *Pill*,
To be another WARD, or HILL,
Before they can obtain their Ends,
To fign Death-warrants for their Friends,
And talents vaft as their's employ,
Secundem Artem to deftroy,
Muft pafs (or Laws their rage reftrain)
Before the Chiefs of *Warwick-Lane*.
Thrice happy *Lane*, where uncontroul'd,
In *Pow'r* and *Lethargy* grown old,
Moft fit to take, in this bleft Land,
The reins which fell from WYNDHAM's hand,
Her lawful throne great DULLNESS rears,
Still more herfelf as more in Years ;
Where She (and who fhall dare deny
Her right, when REEVES and CHAUNCY's by)
Calling to mind, in ancient time,
One GARTH who err'd in Wit and Rime,
Ordains from henceforth to admit
None of the rebel Sons of Wit,
And makes it her peculiar care
That SCHOMBERG never fhall be there.

Not

THE GHOST.

Not fuch as *Thofe*, whom FOLLY trains
To Letters, tho' unblefs'd with brains,
Who deftitute of pow'r and will
To learn, are kept to learning ftill;
Whofe heads, when other methods fail,
Receive inftruction from the tail,
Becaufe their Sires, a common cafe
Which brings the Children to difgrace,
Imagine it a certain rule,
They never could beget a Fool,
Muft pafs, or muft *compound for*, e're
The *Chaplain* full of beef and pray'r,
Will give his *reverend Permit*,
Announcing them for Orders fit,
So that the Prelate (what's a Name?
All Prelates now are much the fame)
May with a confcience fafe and quiet,
With holy hands lay on that *Fiat*,
Which doth all faculties difpenfe,
All Sanctity, all Faith, all Senfe,
Makes MADAN quite a Saint appear,
And makes an Oracle of CHEERE.

Not fuch as in that folemn feat,
Where the *nine Ladies* hold retreat,
The *Ladies nine*, who, as we're told,
Scorning thofe haunts they lov'd of old,
The banks of Isis now prefer,
Nor will one hour from Oxford ftir,
Are held for form ; which Balaam's *Afs*
As well as Balaam's felf might pafs,
And with his Mafter take degrees,
Could he contrive to pay the Fees.

Men of found parts, who, deeply read,
O'erload the Storehoufe of the head
With furniture they ne'er can ufe,
Cannot forgive our rambling Mufe
This wild excurfion ; cannot fee
Why *Phyfic* and *Divinity*,
To the furprize of all beholders,
Are lugg'd in by the head and fhoulders ;
Or how, in any point of view,
Oxford hath any thing to do ;
But Men of nice and fubtle Learning,
Remarkable for quick difcerning,

Thro'

Thro' Spectacles of critic mould,
Without inftruction, will behold
That We a Method here have got,
To fhew What is, by What is not;
And that our drift *(Parenthefis*
For once apart) is briefly this.

Within the brain's moft fecret cells,
A certain *Lord Chief Juftice* dwells
Of fov'reign pow'r, whom One and All,
With common Voice, We REASON call;
Tho', for the purpofes of Satire,
A name in Truth is no great Matter,
JEFFERIES or MANSFIELD, which You will,
It means a *Lord Chief Juftice* ftill.
Here, fo our great Projectors fay,
The Senfes all muft homage pay,
Hither They all muft tribute bring,
And proftrate fall before their King.
Whatever unto them is brought,
Is carry'd on the wings of Thought
Before his throne, where, in full ftate,
He on their merits holds debate,

Examines, Crofs-examines, Weighs
Their right to cenfure or to praife;
Nor doth his equal voice depend
On narrow Views of foe and friend,
Nor can or flattery or force
Divert him from his fteady courfe;
The Channel of Enquiry's clear,
No *fham Examination*'s here.

He, upright Jufticer, no doubt,
Ad libitum puts in and out,
Adjufts and fettles in a trice
What Virtue is, and What is Vice;
What is Perfection, what Defect,
What we muft chufe, and what reject;
He takes upon him to explain
What Pleafure is, and what is Pain,
Whilft We, obedient to the Whim,
And refting all our faith on him,
True Members of the *Stoic* weal,
Muft learn to think, and ceafe to feel.

This glorious Syftem form'd, for Man
To practife when and how he can,

If

If the five Senfes in alliance
To Reafon hurl a proud defiance,
And, tho' oft conquer'd, yet unbroke,
Endeavour to throw off that yoke,
Which they a greater flav'ry hold,
Than Jewifh Bondage was of old ;
Or if They, fomething touch'd with fhame,
Allow him to retain the name
Of Royalty, and, as in Sport,
To hold a mimic formal Court ;
Permitted, no uncommon thing,
To be a kind of Puppet King,
And fuffer'd by the way of toy,
To hold a globe, but not employ ;
Our *Syftem-mongers*, ftruck with fear,
Prognofticate deftruction near ;
All things to Anarchy muft run ;
The little World of Man's undone.

Nay fhould the *Eye*, that niceft Senfe,
Neglect to fend intelligence
Unto the Brain, diftinct and clear,
Of all that paffes in her fphere,

Should

THE GHOST.

Should She prefumptuous joy receive,
Without the Underftanding's leave,
They deem it rank and daring Treafon
Againft the Monarchy of REASON,
Not thinking, tho' they're *wondrous* wife,
That few have *Reafon*, moft have *Eyes*;
So that the Pleafures of the Mind
To a fmall circle are confin'd,
Whilft thofe which to the Senfes fall,
Become the Property of All.
Befides (and this is fure a Cafe
Not much at prefent out of place)
Where NATURE Reafon doth deny,
No Art can that defect fupply,
But if (for it is our intent
Fairly to ftate the argument)
A Man fhould want an eye or two,
The Remedy is fure, tho' new;
The Cure's at hand—no need of Fear—
For proof—behold the CHEVALIER—
As well prepar'd, beyond all doubt,
To put Eyes in, as put them out.

But,

But, Argument apart, which tends
T' embitter foes and fep'rate friends,
(Nor, turn'd apoftate for the *Nine*,
Would I, tho' bred up a Divine,
And foe of courfe to Reafon's weal,
Widen that breach I cannot heal)
By his own Senfe and Feelings taught,
In fpeech as lib'ral as in thought,
Let ev'ry Man enjoy his whim;
What's He to Me, or I to him?
Might I, tho' never rob'd in *Ermine*,
A matter of this weight determine,
No Penalties fhould fettled be
To force men to Hypocrify,
To make them ape an aukward zeal,
And, feeling not, pretend to feel.
I would not have, might fentence reft
Finally fix'd within my breaft,
E'en ANNET cenfur'd and confin'd,
Becaufe we're of a diff'rent mind.

NATURE, who in her act moft free,
Herfelf delights in Liberty,

Profufe

Profufe in Love, and, without bound,
Pours joy on ev'ry creature round;
Whom yet,. was ev'ry bounty fhed
In double Portions on our head,
We could not truly bounteous call,
If FREEDOM did not crown them all.

By Providence forbid to ftray,
Brutes never can miftake their way,
Determin'd ftill, they plod along
By Inftinct, neither right nor wrong;
But Man, had he the heart to ufe
His Freedom, hath a right to chufe,
Whether he acts or well, or ill,
Depends entirely on his will;
To her laft work, her fav'rite Man,
Is giv'n on NATURE's better plan
A Privilege in pow'r to *err*,
Nor let this phrafe refentment ftir
Amongft the grave ones, fince indeed,
The little merit Man can plead
In doing well, dependeth ftill
Upon his pow'r of doing ill.

Opinions

Opinions fhould be free as air;
No man, whate'er his rank, whate'er
His Qualities, a claim can found
That my Opinion muft be bound,
And fquare with his; fuch flavifh chains
From foes the lib'ral foul difdains,
Nor can, tho' true to friendfhip, bend
To wear them even from a friend.
Let Thofe, who rigid Judgment own,
Submiffive bow at Judgment's throne,
And if They of no value hold
Pleafure, till Pleafure is grown cold,
Pall'd and infipid, forc'd to wait
For Judgment's regular debate,
To give it warrant, let them find
Dull Subjects fuited to their mind;
Their's be flow Wifdom; Be *my* plan
To live as merry as I can,
Regardlefs as the fafhions go,
Whether there's Reafon for't, or no;
Be my employment here on earth
To give a lib'ral fcope to mirth,
Life's barren vale with flow'rs t' adorn,
And pluck a rofe from ev'ry thorn.

But

But if, by Error led aftray,
I chance to wander from my way,
Let no blind guide obferve, in fpite,
I'm wrong, who cannot fet me right.
That Doctor could I ne'er endure,
Who found difeafe, and not a cure,
Nor can I hold that man a friend,
Whofe zeal a helping hand fhall lend
To open happy Folly's eyes,
And, making wretched, make me wife;
For next, a Truth which can't admit
Reproof from Wifdom or from Wit,
To *being* happy here below,
Is to *believe* that we are fo.

Some few in *knowledge* find relief,
I place my comfort in *belief*.
Some for *Reality* may call,
FANCY to me is All in All.
Imagination, thro' the trick
Of Doctors, often makes us fick,
And why, let any Sophift tell,
May it not likewife make us well?

This

This am I fure, whate'er our view,
Whatever fhadows we purfue,
For our purfuits, be what they will,
Are little more than fhadows ftill,
Too fwift they fly, too fwift and ftrong,
For man to catch, or hold them long.
But Joys which in the FANCY live, .
. Each moment to each man may give.
True to himfelf, and true to eafe,
He foftens Fate's fevere decrees,
And (can a Mortal wifh for more?)
Creates, and makes himfelf new o'er,
Mocks boafted vain *Reality*,
And *Is*, whate'er he wants to Be.

Hail, FANCY—to thy pow'r I owe
Deliv'rance from the gripe of Woe,
To Thee I owe a mighty debt,
Which Gratitude fhall ne'er forget,
Whilft Mem'ry can her force employ,
A large encreafe of ev'ry joy.
When at my doors, too ftrongly barr'd,
Authority had plac'd a guard,

A

A *knavish* guard, ordain'd by Law

To keep *poor Honesty* in awe;

Authority, severe and stern,

To intercept my wish'd return;

When Foes grew proud, and Friends grew cool,

And Laughter seiz'd each sober fool;

When Candour started in amaze,

And, meaning censure, hinted praise;

When Prudence, lifting up her eyes

And hands, thank'd Heav'n, that she was wise;

When All around Me, with an air

Of hopeless Sorrow, look'd Despair,

When They or said, or seem'd to say,

There is but one, one only way

Better, and be advis'd by us,

Not be at all, than to be thus;

When Virtue shunn'd the shock, and Pride

Disabled, lay by Virtue's side,

Too weak my ruffled soul to chear,

Which could not hope, yet would not fear;

Health in her motion, the wild grace

Of Pleasure speaking in her face,

Dull Regularity thrown by,

And Comfort beaming from her eye,

FANCY,

FANCY, in richeſt robes array'd,
Came ſmiling forth, and brought me aid,
Came ſmiling o'er that dreadful time,
And, more to bleſs me, came in *Rime.*

Nor is her Pow'r to Me confin'd,
It ſpreads, It comprehends Mankind.

When (to the Spirit-ſtirring ſound
Of Trumpets breathing Courage round,
And Fifes, well mingled to reſtrain,
And bring that Courage down again,
Or to the melancholy knell
Of the dull, deep, and doleful bell,
Such as of late the good *Saint Bride*
Muffled, to mortify the pride
Of thoſe, who, ENGLAND quite forgot,
Paid their vile homage to the SCOT,
Where ASGILL held the foremoſt place,
Whilſt my Lord figur'd at a race)
Proceſſions ('tis not worth debate
Whether They are of Stage or State)
Move on, ſo very very ſlow,
'Tis doubtful if they move or no;

When

When the Performers all the while
Mechanically frown or fmile,
Or, with a dull and ftupid ftare,
A vacancy of Senfe declare,
Or, with down-bending eye, feem wrought
Into a Labyrinth of Thought,
Where Reafon wanders ftill in doubt,
And, once got in, cannot get out;
What caufe fufficient can we find
To fatisfy a thinking mind,
Why, dup'd by fuch vain farces, Man
Defcends to act on fuch a plan?
Why They, who hold themfelves divine,
Can in fuch wretched follies join,
Strutting like Peacocks, or like Crows,
Themfelves and *Nature* to expofe?
What Caufe, but that (you'll underftand
We have our Remedy at hand,
That if perchance we ftart a doubt,
Ere it is fix'd, we wipe it out,
As Surgeons, when they lop a limb,
Whether for Profit, Fame, or Whim,
Or mere experiment to try,
Muft always have a *Styptic* by)

FANCY

FANCY fteps in, and ftamps that *real*, ·
Which, *ipfo facto*, is *Ideal*.

Can none remember, yes, I know,
All muft remember that rare fhow,
When to the Country SENSE went down,
And Fools came flocking up to Town;
When *Knights* (a work which all admit
To be for *Knighthood* much unfit)
Built booths for hire; when *Parfons* play'd,
In robes *Canonical* array'd,
And, Fiddling, join'd the *Smithfield* dance,
The price of Tickets to advance;
Or, unto Tapfters turn'd, dealt out,
Running from Booth to Booth about,
To ev'ry Scoundrel, by retail,
True pennyworths of Beef and Ale,
Then firft prepar'd, by bringing beer in,
For prefent grand *Electioneering*;
When *Heralds*, running all about
To bring in Order, turn'd it Out;
When, by the *prudent Marfhal's* care,
Left the rude populace fhould ftare,

And

And with unhallow'd eyes profane
Gay Puppets of Patrician ſtrain,
The whole Proceſſion, as in ſpite,
Unheard, unſeen, ſtole off by Night ;
When our Lov'd Monarch, nothing loth,
Solemnly took that ſacred oath,
Whence mutual firm agreements ſpring
Betwixt the *Subjeꝗ* and the *King*,
By which, in uſual manner crown'd,
His *Head*, his *Heart*, his *Hands* he bound,
Againſt *himſelf*, ſhould Paſſion ſtir
The leaſt Propenſity to err,
Againſt all *Slaves*, who might prepare
Or open force, or hidden ſnare,
That *glorious* CHARTER to maintain,
By which We ſerve, and He muſt reign ;
Then FANCY, with unbounded ſway,
Revell'd ſole Miſtreſs of the day,
And wrought ſuch wonders, as might make
Egyptian Sorcerers forſake
Their baffled mockeries, and own
The Palm of *Magic* Her's alone.

A

A Knight (who in the filken lap
Of lazy Peace, had liv'd on Pap,
Who never yet had dar'd to roam
'Bove ten or twenty miles from home,
Nor even that, unlefs a *Guide*
Was plac'd to amble by his fide,
And troops of Slaves were fpread around
To keep his Honour fafe and found,
Who could not fuffer for his life
A Point to fword, or Edge to knife,
And always fainted at the fight
Of Blood, tho' 'twas not fhed in fight,
Who difinherited one Son
For firing off an *Elder* Gun,
And whipt another, fix years old,
Becaufe the Boy, prefumptuous, bold
To Madnefs, likely to become
A very Swifs, had beat a drum,
Tho' it appear'd an inftrument
Moft *peaceable* and *innocent*,
Having from firft been in the hands
And fervice of the *City Bands)*
Grac'd with thofe enfigns, which were meant
To further Honour's dread intent,

The

THE GHOST.

The Minds of Warriors to inflame,
And fpur them on to deeds of Fame,
With little Sword, large Spurs, high Feather,
Fearful of ev'ry thing but Weather,
(And all muft own, who pay regard
To Charity, it had been hard
That in his very firft *Campaign*
His *Honours* fhould be foil'd with rain)
A Hero all at once became,
And (feeing others much the fame
In point of Valour as himfelf,
Who leave their Courage on a fhelf
From Year to Year, till fome fuch rout
In proper feafon calls it out)
Strutted, look'd big, and fwagger'd more
Than ever Hero did before,
Look'd up, Look'd down, Look'd all around,
Like MAVORS, grimly fmil'd and frown'd,
Seem'd Heav'n, and Earth, and Hell to call
To fight, that he might rout them all,
And perfonated Valour's ftile
So long, Spectators to beguile,
That paffing ftrange, and wondrous true,
Himfelf at laft believ'd it too,

Nor

Nor for a time could he difcern,
Till Truth and Darkneſs took their turn,
So well did FANCY play her part,
That Coward ſtill was at the heart.

WHIFFLE (who knows not WHIFFLE's name,
By the impartial voice of fame
Recorded firſt, thro' all this land,
In Vanity's illuſtrious band?)
Who, by all bounteous Nature meant
For offices of hardiment,
A modern HERCULES at leaſt,
To rid the world of each wild beaſt,
Of each wild beaſt which came in view,
Whether on four legs or on two,
Degenerate, delights to prove
His force on the *Parade* of Love,
Difclaims the joys which camps afford,
And for the Diſtaff quits the ſword;
Who fond of women would appear
To public eye, and public ear,
But, when in private, let's them know
How little they can truſt to ſhow;

Who

Who sports a Woman, as of courfe,
Just as a Jockey shews a horfe,
And then returns her to the ftable,
Or vainly plants her at his table,
Where he would rather VENUS find,
(So pall'd, and so deprav'd his mind)
Than, by fome great occafion led,
To feize Her panting in her bed,
Burning with more than mortal fires,
And melting in her own defires;
Who, ripe in years, is yet a child,
Thro' fafhion, not thro' feeling wild;
Whate'er in others, who proceed
As Senfe and Nature have decreed,
From real paffion flows, in him
Is mere effect of mode and whim;
Who Laughs, a very common way,
Becaufe he nothing has to fay,
As your *choice* SPIRITS oaths difpenfe
To fill up vacancies of Senfe;
Who, having fome fmall Senfe, defies't,
Or, ufing, always mifapplies it;
Who now and then brings fomething forth,
Which feems indeed of Sterling Worth,

                              Something,

Something, by fudden Start and Fit,
Which at a diftance looks like wit,
But, on Examination near,
To his confufion will appear
By Truth's fair glafs, to be at beft
A Threadbare Jefter's threadbare jeft;
Who frifks and dances thro' the ftreet,
Sings without voice, rides without feat,
Plays o'er his tricks, like Æsop's Afs,
A *gratis* fool to all who pafs;
Who riots, tho' he loves not wafte,
Whores without luft, drinks without tafte,
Acts without fenfe, talks without thought,
Does every thing but what he ought;
Who, led by forms, without the pow'r
Of Vice, is Vicious; who one hour,
Proud without Pride, the next will be
Humble without Humility;
Whofe Vanity we all difcern,
The Spring on which his actions turn;
Whofe aim in erring, is to err,
So that he may be fingular,
And all his utmoft wifhes mean,
Is, tho' he's laugh'd at, to be feen,

Such

Such (for when FLATT'RY's foothing ftrain
Had robb'd the Mufe of her difdain,
And found a method to perfuade
Her art, to foften ev'ry fhade,
JUSTICE enrag'd, the pencil fnatch'd
From her degen'rate hand, and fcratch'd
Out ev'ry trace; then, quick as thought,
From life this ftriking likenefs caught)
In Mind, in Manners, and in Mien,
Such WHIFFLE came, and fuch was feen
In the World's eye, but (ftrange to tell!)
Mifled by FANCY's magic fpell,
Deceiv'd, not dreaming of deceit,
Cheated, but happy in the cheat,
Was more than human in his own.
O bow, bow All at FANCY's throne,
Whofe Pow'r could make fo vile an Elf,
With Patience bear that thing, *himfelf.*

But, Miftrefs of each art to pleafe,
Creative FANCY, what are thefe,
Thefe Pageants of a trifler's Pen,
To what thy Pow'r effected then?

Familiar

Familiar with the human mind,
As swift and subtle as the wind,
Which we all feel, yet no one knows
Or whence it comes, or where it goes,
FANCY at *once* in ev'ry part
Possess'd the Eye, the Head, the Heart,
And in a thousand forms array'd,
A thousand various gambols play'd.

Here, in a Face which well might ask
The Privilege to wear a mask
In spite of Law, and Justice teach
For public good t' excuse the breach,
Within the furrow of a wrinkle
'Twixt Eyes, which could not shine but twinkle,
Like Centinels i' th' starry way,
Who wait for the return of day,
Almost burnt out, and seem to keep
Their watch, like Soldiers, in their sleep,
Or like those lamps which, by the pow'r
Of Law, must burn from hour to hour,
(Else they, without redemption, fall
Under the terrors of that Hall,

Which,

Which, once notorious for a *hop*,
Is now become *a Juftice-fhop)*
Which are fo manag'd, to go out
Juft when the time comes round about,
Which yet thro' emulation ftrive
To keep their dying light alive, .
And (not uncommon, as we find,
Amongft the children of mankind)
As they grow weaker, would feem ftronger,
And burn a little, little longer;
FANCY, betwixt fuch'eyes enfhrin'd,
No brufh to daub, no mill to grind,
Thrice wav'd her wand around, whofe force
Chang'd in an inftant Nature's courfe,
And, hardly credible in Rime,
Not only ftopp'd, but call'd back Time.
The Face of ev'ry wrinkle clear'd,
Smooth as the floating ftream appear'd,
Down the Neck ringlets fpread their flame,
The Neck admiring whence they came; .
On the Arch'd Brow the *Graces* play'd ;
On the full Bofom *Cupid* laid ;
Suns, from their proper orbits fent,
Became for Eyes a fupplement;

                                        Teeth,

Teeth, white as ever Teeth were seen
Deliver'd from the hand of GREEN,
Started, in regular array,
Like Train-Bands on a grand Field-day,
Into the Gums, which would have fled,
But, wond'ring, turn'd from white to red,
Quite alter'd was the whole machine,
And Lady ——— ——— was fifteen.

Here She made lordly temples rife
Before the pious DASHWOOD's eyes,
Temples which built aloft in air,
May ferve for fhow, if not for pray'r;
In folemn form Herfelf, before,
Array'd like *Faith*, the *Bible* bore.
There, over MELCOMB's feather'd head,
Who, quite a man of Gingerbread,
Savour'd in talk, in drefs, and phyz,
More of another World than this,
To a *dwarf Mufe a Giant Page*,
The laft grave Fop of the laft Age,
In a fuperb and feather'd hearfe,
Befcutcheon'd and *betagg'd* with Verfe,

G 4 Which,

Which, to Beholders from afar,
Appear'd like a triumphal Car,
She rode, in a *caſt* Rainbow clad ;
There, throwing off the *hallow'd plaid*,
Naked, as when (in thoſe drear Cells
Where, *Self-bleſs'd*, *Self-curs'd* MADNESS dwells)
PLEASURE, on whom, in *Laughter*'s ſhape,
FRENZY had perfected a rape,
Firſt brought her forth, before her time,
Wild Witneſs of her ſhame and crime,
Driving before an Idol band
Of driv'ling STUARTS, hand in hand,
Some, who to curſe Mankind, had Wore
A Crown they ne'er muſt think of more,
Others, whoſe baby brows were grac'd
With Paper Crowns, and Toys of Paſte,
She Jigg'd, and playing on the Flute
Spread raptures o'er the ſoul of BUTE.

Big with vaſt hopes, ſome mighty plan,
Which wrought the buſy ſoul of man
To her full bent, the CIVIL LAW,
Fit *Code* to keep a world in awe,

Bound o'er his brows, fair to behold,
As *Jewish Frontlets* were of old,
The famous CHARTER of our land,
Defac'd, and mangled in his hand;
As one whom deepest thoughts employ,
But deepest thoughts of truest joy,
Serious and flow he strode, he stalk'd,
Before him troops of Heroes walk'd,
Whom best He lov'd, of Heroes crown'd,
By TORIES guarded all around,
Dull solemn pleasure in his face,
He saw the honours of his race,
He saw their lineal glories rise,
And touch'd, or seem'd to touch the skies.
Not the most distant mark of fear,
No sign of *axe*, or *scaffold* near,
Not one curs'd thought, to cross his will,
Of such a place as *Tower Hill.*

Curse on this *Muse*, a flippant Jade,
A Shrew, like ev'ry other Maid
Who turns the corner of nineteen,
Devour'd with peevishness and spleen.

Her

Her Tongue (for as, when bound for life,
The Hufband fuffers for the Wife,
So if in any works of rime
Perchance there blunders out a crime,
Poor Culprit Bards muft always rue it,
Altho' 'tis plain the Mufes do it)
Sooner or later cannot fail
To fend me headlong to a jail.
Whate'er my theme (our themes we chufe
In modern days without a *Mufe,*
Juft as a Father will provide
To join a Bridegroom and a Bride,
As if, tho' they muft be the Play'rs,
The game was wholly *his,* not *theirs*)
Whate'er my theme, the *Mufe,* who ftill
Owns no direction but her will,
Flies off, and, ere I could expect,
By ways oblique and indirect,
At once quite over head and ears,
In fatal *Politics* appears.
Time was, and, if I ought difcern
Of fate, that Time fhall foon return,
When *decent* and *demure* at leaft,
As grave and dull as any Prieft,

I could

I could fee *Vice* in robes array'd,
Could fee the game of *Folly* play'd
Succefsfully in Fortune's fchool,
Without exclaiming rogue or fool;
Time was, when nothing loth or proud,
I lacquied, with the fawning crowd,
Scoundrels in Office, and would bow
To Cyphers great in place ; but now
Upright I ftand, as if wife Fate,
To compliment a fhatter'd ftate,
Had me, like ATLAS, hither fent
To fhoulder up the firmament,
And if I ftoop'd, with gen'ral crack
The Heavens would tumble from my back;
Time was, when rank and fituation
Secur'd the great Ones of the Nation
From all controul ; *Satire* and *Law*
Kept only little Knaves in awe,
But now, *Decorum* loft, I ftand
Bemus'd, a Pencil in my hand,
And, dead to ev'ry fenfe of fhame,
Carelefs of Safety and of Fame,
The names of Scoundrels minute down,
And Libel more than half the Town.

How

How can a Statefman be fecure
In all his Villainies, if poor
And dirty Authors thus fhall dare
To lay his rotten bofom bare?
Mufes fhould pafs away their time,
In drefling out the Poet's rime
With Bills and Ribbands, and array
Each line in harmlefs tafte, tho' gay.
When the hot burning Fit is on,
They fhould regale their reftlefs Son
With fomething to allay his rage,
Some cool Caftalian Beverage,
Or fome fuch draught (tho' *They*, 'tis plain,
Taking the Mufes name in vain,
Know nothing of their real court,
And only fable from report)
As makes a WHITEHEAD's *Ode* go down,
Or flakes the *Feverette* of *Brown*:
Eut who would in his Senfes think
Of Mufes giving gall to drink,
Or that their folly fhould afford
To raving Poets Gun or Sword?
Poets were ne'er defign'd by fate
To meddle with affairs of State,

Nor

Nor ſhould (if we may ſpeak our thought
Truely as men of Honour ought)
Sound Policy their rage admit,
To Launch the thunderbolts of Wit
About thoſe heads, which, when they're ſhot,
Can't tell if 'twas by Wit, or not.

Theſe things well known, what Devil in ſpite
Can have ſeduc'd me thus to write
Out of that road, which muſt have led
To riches, without heart or head,
Into that road, which, had I more
Than ever Poet had before,
Of Wit and Virtue, in diſgrace
Would keep me ſtill, and out of place,
Which, if ſome *Judge* (You'll underſtand
One famous, famous thro' the land
For *making* Law) ſhould ſtand my friend,
At laſt may in a Pill'ry end,
And all this, I my ſelf admit,
Without one cauſe to lead to it.——

For inſtance now—this book—the GHOST—
Methinks I hear ſome Critic Poſt

Remark

Remark moſt gravely—" The firſt word
Which we about the Ghoſt have heard."
Peace, my good Sir—not quite ſo faſt—
What is the firſt, may be the laſt,
Which is a point, all muſt agree,
Cannot depend on You or Me.
FANNY, no Ghoſt of common mould,
Is not by forms to be controul'd,
To keep her ſtate, and ſhew her ſkill,
She never comes but when ſhe will.
I wrote and wrote (perhaps you doubt,
And ſhrewdly, what I wrote about,
Believe me, much to my diſgrace,
I too am in the ſelf-ſame caſe)
But ſtill I wrote, till FANNY came
Impatient, nor could any ſhame
On me with equal juſtice fall,
If She had never come at all.
An Underling, I could not ſtir
Without the Cue thrown out by her,
Nor from the ſubjeƈt aid receive
Until She came, and gave me leave.
So that (Ye Sons of Erudition
Mark, this is but a ſuppoſition,

Nor

Nor would I to fo wife a nation
Suggeft it as a *Revelation*)
If henceforth dully turning o'er
Page after Page, Ye read no more
Of FANNY, who, in Sea or Air,
May be departed God knows where,
Rail at jilt Fortune, but agree
No cenfure can be laid on me,
For fure (the caufe let MANSFIELD try)
FANNY is in the fault, not I.

But to return—and this I hold,
A fecret worth its weight in gold
To thofe who write, as I write now,
Not to mind where they go, or how,
Thro' ditch, thro' bog, o'er hedge and ftile,
Make it but worth the Reader's while,
And keep a paffage fair and plain
Always to bring him back again.
Thro' dirt, who fcruples to approach,
At pleafure's call to take a coach,
But we fhould think the man a clown
Who in the dirt fhould fet us down?

But to return—if WIT, who ne'er
The fhackles of reftraint could bear,
In wayward humour fhould refufe
Her timely fuccour to the *Mufe*,
And to no rules and orders tied,
Roughly deny to be her guide,
She muft renounce *Decorum*'s plan,
And get back when, and how fhe can,
As *Parfons*, who, without pretext,
As foon as mention'd, quit their text,
And, to promote Sleep's genial pow'r,
Grope in the dark for half an Hour,
Give no more Reafon (for we know
Reafon is vulgar, mean, and low)
Why they come back (fhould it befal
That ever they come back at all)
Into the road, to end the rout,
Than they can give Why they went out.

But to return—this Book—the GHOST—
A mere amufement at the moft,
A trifle, fit to wear away
The horrors of a rainy day,

A flight

A flight fhot filk, for fummer wear,
Juft as our modern State men are,
If rigid honefty permit
That I for once purloin the Wit
Of him, who, were we all to fteal,
Is much too rich the theft to feel.
Yet in this Book, where Eafe fhould join
With Mirth to *fugar* ev'ry line,
Where it fhould all be mere *Chit Chat*,
Lively, Good humour'd, and *all that*,
Where *honeft* SATIRE, in difgrace,
Should not fo much as fhew her face,
The Shrew, o'erleaping all due bounds,
Breaks into Laughter's facred grounds,
And, in contempt, plays o'er her tricks
In *Science, Trade,* and *Politics.*

But why fhould the diftemper'd Scold
Attempt to blacken Men enroll'd
In Pow'r's dread book, whofe mighty fkill
Can twift an Empire to their will,
Whofe Voice is Fate, and on their tongue
Law, Liberty, and *Life* are hung,

Whom on enquiry, Truth fhall find,
With STUARTS *link'd,* time out of mind
Superior to their Country's Laws,
Defenders of a Tyrant's caufe,
Men, who the fame damn'd maxims hold
Darkly, which they avow'd of old,
Who, tho' by diff'rent means, purfue
The end which they had firft in view,
And, force found vain, now play their part
With much lefs Honour, much more Art?
Why, at the Corners of the Streets,
To ev'ry Patriot drudge She meets,
Known or unknown, with furious cry
Should She wild clamours vent, or why,
The minds of *Groundlings* to inflame,
A DASHWOOD, BUTE, and WYNDHAM name?
Why, having not to our furprize
The fear of death before her Eyes,
Bearing, and that but now and then,
No other weapon but her pen,
Should She an argument afford,
For blood, to Men who *wear a fword,*
Men, who can nicely *trim* and *pare*
A point of HONOUR to a hair,

(HONOUR

(HONOUR—a Word of nice import,
A pretty trinket in a Court,
Which *my Lord* quite in rapture feels
Dangling, and rattling with his Seals—
HONOUR—a Word, which all the *Nine*
Would be much puzzled to define—
HONOUR—a Word which torture mocks
And might confound a thoufand LOCKES—
Which (for I leave to wifer heads,
Who fields of death prefer to beds
Of down, to find out, if they can
What HONOUR *is*, on their Wild plan)
Is *not*, to take it in their Way,
And this we fure may dare to fay
Without incurring an offence,
Courage, Law, Honefty, or *Senfe)*
Men, who all Spirit, Life and Soul,
Neat Butchers of a *Button-hole,*
Having more fkill, believe it true
That they muft have more courage too,
Men, who without a place or name,
Their Fortunes fpeechlefs as their fame,
Would by the Sword new Fortunes carve,
And rather die in fight than ftarve?

At *Coronations*, a vaft field
Which food of ev'ry kind might yield,
Of good found food, at once moft fit
For purpofes of health and wit,
Could not ambitious SATIRE reft,
Content with what fhe might digeft?
Could fhe not feaft on things of courfe,
A *Champion*, or a Champion's *horfe*?
A Champion's *horfe*—no, better fay,
Tho' better figur'd on that day—
A *horfe*, which might appear to us,
Who deal in rime, a PEGASUS,
A *Rider*, who, when once got on,
Might pafs for a BELLEROPHON,
Dropt on a fudden from the fkies,
To catch and fix our wond'ring eyes,
To witch, with wand inftead of whip,
The world with *noble* horfemanfhip,
To twift and twine, both Horfe and Man,
On fuch a well-concerted plan,
That, *Centaur*-like, when all was done,
We fcarce could think they were not one?
Could She not to our itching ears
Bring the new names of *new-coin'd* Peers,

Who

Who Walk'd, Nobility forgot,
With fhoulders fitter for a knot,
Than robes of Honour, for whofe fake
Heralds in form were forc'd to make,
To make, becaufe they could not find,
Great Predeceffors to their mind?
Could She not (tho' 'tis doubtful fince
Whether He *Plumber* is, or *Prince)*
Tell of a fimple Knight's advance
To be a doughty Peer of *France,*
Tell how he did a Dukedom gain,
And ROBINSON was AQUITAIN,
Tell how her City-Chiefs difgrac'd,
Were at an empty table plac'd,
A grofs neglect, which, whilft they live,
They can't forget, and won't forgive,
A grofs neglect of all thofe rights
Which march with City Appetites,
Of all thofe Canons, which we find
By *Gluttony,* time out of mind,
Eftablifh'd; which they ever hold,
Dearer than any thing but Gold?

H 3   Thanks

Thanks to my Stars—I now see shore—
Of Courtiers, and of Courts no more—
Thus stumbling on my City Friends,
Blind Chance my guide, my purpose bends
In line direct, and shall pursue
The point which I had first in view,
Nor more shall with the reader sport
Till I have seen him safe in port.
Hush'd be each fear—no more I bear
Thro' the wide regions of the air
The Reader terrified, no more
Wild Ocean's horrid paths explore.
Be the plain track from henceforth mine—
Cross-roads to ALLEN I resign,
ALLEN, the honour of this nation,
ALLEN, himself a *Corporation*,
ALLEN, of late notorious grown
For writings none, or all his own,
ALLEN, the first of *letter'd* men,
Since the *good* Bishop holds his pen,
And at his elbow takes his stand
To mend his head, and guide his hand.
But hold—once more *Digression* hence—
Let us return to *Common Sense*,

                                      The

The Car of PHOEBUS I difcharge;
My Carriage now a LORD-MAYOR's *Barge*.

Suppofe we now—we may fuppofe
In Verfe, what would be Sin in Profe—
The Sky with darknefs overfpread,
And ev'ry Star retir'd to bed,
The gew-gaw robes of Pomp and Pride
In fome dark corner thrown afide,
Great *Lords* and *Ladies* giving way
To what they feem to fcorn by day,
The real feelings of the heart,
And Nature taking place of Art,
Defire triumphant thro' the Night,
And *Beauty* panting with delight,
Chaftity, Woman's faireft crown,
Till the return of Morn laid down,
Then to be worn again as bright
As if not fullied in the Night,
Dull *Ceremony*, bufinefs o'er,
Dreaming in form at COTTRELL's door,
Precaution trudging all about
To fee the Candles fafely out,

Bearing

Bearing a mighty *Mafter Key*,
Habited like *Oeconomy*, ˋ
Stamping each lock with triple feals,
Mean Av'rice creeping at her heels.

　Suppofe we too, like fheep in Pen,
The *Mayor* and *Court of Aldermen*
Within their barge, which thro' the deep,
The Rowers more than half afleep,
Mov'd flow, as over-charg'd with State;
Thames groan'd beneath the mighty weight,
And felt that *bawble* heavier far　•
Than a whole fleet of men of war.
Sleep o'er each well-known faithful head
With lib'ral hand his Poppies fhed,
Each head, by Dullness rend'red fit
Sleep and his Empire to admit.
Thro' the whole paffage not a word,
Not one faint, weak, half found was heard;
Sleep had prevail'd to overwhelm
The Steerfman nodding o'er the helm;
The Rowers, without force or fkill,
Left the dull Barge to drive at will;

The

The fluggifh Oars fufpended hung,
And even BEARDMORE held his *tongue*.
COMMERCE, regardful of a freight,
On which depended half her *State*,
Stepp'd to the helm, with ready hand
She fafely clear'd that bank of Sand,
Where, ftranded, our Weft-Country Fleet
Delay and Danger often meet;
Till NEPTUNE, anxious for the trade,
Comes in full tides, and brings them aid;
Next (for the Mufes can furvey
Objects by Night as well as day,
Nothing prevents their taking aim,
Darknefs and Light to them the fame)
They paft that building, which of old
Queen-mothers was defign'd to hold,
At prefent a mere *lodging-pen*,
A Palace turn'd into a den,
To Barracks turn'd, and Soldiers tread
Where *Dowagers* have laid their head;
Why fhould we mention *Surrey-Strect*,
Where ev'ry week grave Judges meet,
All fitted out with *hum* and *ba*,
In proper form to drawl out Law,

To fee all caufes duly tried

'Twixt Knaves who drive, and Fools who ride ?

Why at the *Temple* fhould we ftay ?

What of the *Temple* dare we fay ?

A dang'rous ground we tread on there,

And words perhaps may actions bear,

Where, as the Breth'ren of the feas

For *fares*, the Lawyers ply for fees.

What of that *Bridge*, moft wifely made

To ferve the purpofes of trade,

In the great Mart of all this Nation,

By ftopping up the Navigation,

And to that Sand-bank adding weight,

Which is already much too great ?—

What of that *Bridge*, which, void of Senfe,

But well fupplied with impudence,

Englifhmen, knowing not the *Guild*,

Thought they might have a claim to build,

Till PATERSON, as white as milk,

As fmooth as oil, as foft as filk,

In folemn manner had decreed,

That, on the other fide the TWEED,

ART, born and bred, and fully grown,

Was with one MYLNE, a man unknown,

But

But grace, preferment, and renown
Deserving, just arriv'd in town;
One MYLNE, an Artist perfect quite,
Both in his own, and country's right,
As fit to make a bridge, as He,
With glorious *Patavinity*,
To build inscriptions, worthy found
To lie for ever under ground.

    Much more, worth observation too,
Was this a season to pursue
The theme, Our Muse might tell in rime;
The Will She hath, but not the time;
For, swift as shaft from Indian bow,
(And when a Goddess comes, we know,
Surpassing Nature acts prevail,
And boats want neither oar, nor sail)
The Vessel past, and reach'd the shore
So quick, that Thought was scarce before.

    Suppose we now our *City-Court*
Safely deliver'd at the port,
And, of their State regardless quite,
Landed, like smuggled goods, by night;

The

The folemn Magiftrate laid down,
The dignity of robe and gown
With ev'ry other enfign gone ;
Suppofe the woollen Night-Cap on :
The *Flefh-brufh* us'd with decent ftate
To make the Spirits circulate,
(A form, which to the Senfes true,
The liq'rifh Chaplain ufes too,
Tho', fomething to Improve the plan,
He takes the Maid inftead of Man)
Swath'd, and with flannel cover'd o'er
To fhew the vigour of thréefcore,
The vigour of threefcore and ten
Above the proof of younger men,
Suppofe, the mighty Dullman led
Betwixt two flaves, and put to bed ;
Suppofe, the moment he lies down,
No miracle in this great town,
The Drone as faft afleep, as He
Muft in the courfe of Nature be,
Who, truth for our foundation take,
When up, is never half awake.

There

There let him fleep, whilft we furvey
The preparations for the day,
That day, on which was to be fhewn
Court-Pride by *City Pride* outdone.

The jealous Mother fends away,
As only fit for childifh play,
That Daughter, who, to gall her pride,
Shoots up too forward by her fide.

The *Wretch*, of God and man accurs'd,
Of all Hell's inftruments the worft,
Draws forth his *pawns*, and for the day
Struts in fome Spendthrift's vain array;
Around his aukward doxy fhine
The treafures of GOLCONDA's mine,
Each Neighbour, with a jealous glare,
Beholds her folly publifh'd there.

Garments, well fav'd (an anecdote
Which we can prove, or would not quote)
Garments well-fav'd, which firft were made,
When Taylors, to promote their Trade,

Againft

Againſt the *Piɛ̃ts* in arms aroſe,
And drove them out, or made them cloaths;
Garments, immortal, without end,
Like Names, and Titles, which deſcend
Succeſſively from Sire to Son;
Garments, unleſs ſome work is done
Of Note, not ſuffer'd to appear
'Bove once at moſt in ev'ry year,
Were now, in ſolemn form, laid bare
To take the benefit of air,
And, ere they came to be employ'd
On this Solemnity, to void
That ſcent, which RUSSIA's leather gave,
From vile and impious Moth to ſave.

Each head was buſy, and each heart
In preparation bore a part.
Running together all about
The Servants put each other out,
Till the grave Maſter had decreed,
The more haſte, ever the worſe ſpeed;
Miſs, with her little eyes half-clos'd,
Over a ſmuggled toilet dos'd;

The

The *Waiting-Maid*, whom Story notes
A very *Scrub* in petticoats,
Hir'd for one Work, but doing all,
In flumbers lean'd againft the wall;
Milliners, fummon'd from afar,
Arriv'd in fhoals at *Temple-bar*,
Strictly commanded to import
Cart-loads of foppery from Court;
With labour'd vifible defign
ART ftrove to be *fuperbly* fine,
NATURE, more pleafing, tho' more wild,
Taught otherwife her *darling* child,
And cried, with fpirited difdain,
Be H—— elegant and plain.

Lo! from the chambers of the Eaft,
A welcome prelude to the feaft,
In *faffron-colour'd* robe array'd,
High in a Car by VULCAN made,
Who work'd for JOVE himfelf, each Steed
High mettled, of celeftial breed,
Pawing and Pacing all the way,
AURORA brought the wifh'd-for day,

And held her empire, till out-run
By that brave jolly groom the SUN.

The Trumpet—hark! It fpeaks—It fwells
The loud full harmony, It tells
The time at hand, when DULLMAN, led
By form, his Citizens muft head,
And march thofe troops, which at his call
Were now affembled, to *Guild-Hall*,
On matters of importance great
To *Court* and *City*, *Church* and *State*.

From end to end the found makes way,
All hear the Signal and obey,
But DULLMAN, who, his charge forgot,
By MORPHEUS fetter'd, heard it not;
Nor could, fo found he flept and faft,
Hear any Trumpet, but the laft.

CRAPE, ever true and trufty known,
Stole from the Maid's bed to his own,
Then in the Spirituals of pride,
Planted himfelf at DULLMAN's fide.

Thrice

Thrice did the ever-faithful Slave,
With voice which might have reach'd the grave,
And broke death's adamantine chain,
On DULLMAN call, but call'd in vain;
Thrice with an arm, which might have made
The THEBAN Boxer curse his trade,
The drone he shook, who rear'd the head,
And *thrice* fell backward on his bed.
What could be done? where force hath fail'd,
Policy often hath prevail'd,
And what, an inference most plain,
Had been, CRAPE thought might be again.

Under his pillow (still in mind
The Proverb kept, *fast bind, fast find)*
Each blessed night the keys were laid,
Which CRAPE to draw away assay'd.
What not the pow'r of voice or arm
Could do, this did, and broke the charm;
Quick started He with stupid stare,
For all his little Soul was there.

Behold him, taken up, rubb'd down,
In Elbow-Chair, and Morning-Gown;

Behold him, in his latter bloom,
Stripp'd, wafh'd, and fprinkled with perfume;
Behold him bending with the weight
Of Robes, and trumpery of State;
Behold him (for the Maxim's true,
Whate'er we by another do,
We do ourfelves, and Chaplain paid,
Like flaves, in ev'ry other trade,
Had mutter'd over God knows what,
Something which he by heart had got)
Having, as ufual, faid his pray'rs,
Go *titter*, *totter*, to the ftairs;
Behold him for defcent prepare,
With one foot trembling in the air;
He *ftarts*, he *paufes* on the brink,
And, hard to credit, feems to *think*;
Thro' his whole train (the Chaplain gave
The proper cue to ev'ry flave)
At once, as with infection caught,
Each *ftarted*, *paus'd*, and *aim'd* at thought;
He turns, and they turn; big with care,
He waddles to his Elbow-Chair,
Squats down, and, filent for a feafon,
At laft with CRAPE begins to reafon;

But

But firſt of all he made a ſign
That ev'ry ſoul, but the *Divine*,
Should quit the room ; in him, he knows,
He may all confidence repoſe.

CRAPE—tho' I'm yet not quite awake—
Before this awful ſtep I take,
On which my future all depends,
I ought to know my foes and friends.
By foes and friends, obſerve me ſtill,
I mean not thoſe who well, or ill
Perhaps may wiſh me, but thoſe who
Have't in their power to do it too.
Now if, attentive to the State,
In too much hurry to be great,
Or thro' much zeal, a motive, CRAPE,
Deſerving praiſe, into a ſcrape
I, like a Fool, am got, no doubt,
I, like a Wiſe Man, ſhould get out.
Not that, remark without replies,
I ſay that to get out is wiſe,
Or, by the very ſelf-ſame rule
That to get in was like a Fool ;

The

The marrow of this argument
Muft wholly reft on the event,
And therefore, which is really hard,
Againft events too I muft guard.

Should things continue as they *ftand*,
And BUTE prevail thro' all the land
Without a rival, by his aid,
My fortunes in a trice are made;
Nay, Honours on my zeal may finile,
And ftamp me Earl of fome great Ifle;
But, if a matter of much doubt,
The prefent Minifter goes out,
Fain would I know on what pretext
I can ftand fairly with the next?
For as my aim at ev'ry hour
Is to be well with thofe in pow'r,
And my material point of view,
Whoever's in, to be in too,
I fhould not, like a blockhead, chufe
To gain *thefe* fo as *thofe* to lofe;
'Tis good in ev'ry cafe, You know,
To have two ftrings unto our bow.

As

As one in wonder loft, CRAPE view'd
His Lord, who thus his fpeech purfued.

This, my good CRAPE, is my grand point,
And, as the times are out of joint,
The greater caution is requir'd
To bring about the point defir'd.
What I would wifh to bring about
Cannot admit a moment's doubt;
The matter in difpute, You know,
Is what we call the *quomodo.*
That be thy tafk—The *Rev'rend* Slave,
Becoming in a moment grave,
Fixt to the ground and rooted ftood,
Juft like a man cut out of wood,
Such as we fee (without the leaft
Reflection glancing on the Prieft)
One or more, planted up and down,
Almoft in ev'ry Church in town;
He ftood fome minutes, then, like one
Who wifh'd the matter might be done,
But could not do it, fhook his head,
And thus the man of Sorrow faid:

Hard

Hard is this taſk, too hard I ſwear,
By much too hard for me to bear,
Beyond expreſſion hard my part,
Could mighty DULLMAN ſee my heart,
When He, alas! makes known a will,
Which CRAPE's not able to fulfil.
Was ever my obedience barr'd
By any trifling nice regard
To Senſe and Honour? could I reach
Thy meaning without help of ſpeech,
At the firſt motion of thy eye
Did not thy faithful creature fly?
Have I not ſaid, not what I ought,
But what by earthly Maſter taught?
Did I e'er weigh, thro' duty ſtrong,
In thy great biddings, right and wrong?
Did ever Int'reſt, to whom Thou
Can'ſt not with more devotion bow,
Warp my ſound faith, or will of mine
In contradiction run to thine?
Have I not, at thy table plac'd,
When buſineſs call'd aloud for haſte,
Torn myſelf thence, yet never heard
To utter one complaining word,

And

And had, till thy great work was done,
All appetites, as having none ?
Hard is it, this great plan purfu'd
Of Voluntary fervitude,
Purfued, without or fhame or fear,
Thro' the great circle of the Year ;
Now to receive, in this grand hour,
Commands which lie beyond my pow'r ;
Commands which baffile all my fkill,
And leave me nothing but my will :
Be that accepted ; let my Lord
Indulgence to his flave afford ;
This Tafk, for my poor ftrength unfit,
Will yield to none but DULLMAN's wit.

With fuch grofs incenfe gratified,
And turning up the lip of pride,
Poor CRAPE—and fhook his empty head—
Poor puzzled CRAPE, wife DULLMAN faid,
Of judgment weak, of fenfe confin'd,
For things of lower note defign'd,
For things within the vulgar reach,
To run *of* errands, and to preach,

Well

Well haft Thou judg'd, that heads like mine
Cannot want help from heads like thine ;
Well haft Thou judg'd thyfelf unmeet
Of fuch high argument to treat ;
'Twas but to try thee that I fpoke,
And all I faid was but a joke.

Nor think a joke, CRAPE, a difgrace
Or to my Perfon, or my place ;
The wifeft of the Sons of Men
Have deign'd to ufe them now and then.
The only caution, do You fee,
Demanded by our dignity,
From common ufe and men exempt,
Is that they may not breed contempt.
Great Ufe they have, when in the hands
Of One, like me, who underftands,
Who underftands the time and place,
The perfons, manner, and the grace,
Which Fools neglect ; fo that we find,
If all the requifitcs are join'd,
From whence a perfect joke muft fpring,
A joke's a very ferious thing.

                                        But

But to our bufinefs—my defign,
Which gave fo rough a fhock to thine,
To my Capacity is made
As ready as a fraud in trade,
Which, like Broad-Cloth, I can, with eafe,
Cut out in any fhape I pleafe.

Some, in my circumftance, fome few,
Aye, and thofe men of Genius too,
Good Men, who, without Love or Hate,
Whether they early rife or late,
With names uncrack'd, and credit found,
Rife worth a hundred thoufand pound,
By *threadbare* ways and means would try
To bear their point—fo will not I.
New methods fhall my wifdom find
To fuit thefe matters to my mind,
So that the Infidels at Court,
Who make our City Wits their fport,
Shall hail the honours of my reign,
And own that DULLMAN bears a brain.

Some, in my place, to gain their ends,
Would give relations up, and friends;

Would

Would lend a wife, who they might fwear
Safely, was none the worfe for wear;
Would fee a Daughter, yet a maid,
Into a Statefman's arms betray'd,
Nay, fhould the Girl prove coy, nor know
What Daughters to a Father owe,
Sooner than fchemes fo nobly plann'd
Should fail, themfelves would lend a hand;
Would vote on one fide, whilft a brother,
Properly taught, would vote on t'other;
Would ev'ry petty band forget;
To public eye be with *one* fet,
In private with a *fecond* herd,
And be by Proxy with a *third*;
Would (like a *Queen*, of whom I read
The other day—her name is fled—
In a book (where, together bound,
WHITTINGTON and his CAT I found,
A tale moft true, and free from art,
Which all LORD-MAYORS fhould have by heart)
A *Queen* (O might thofe days begin
Afrefh when Queens would learn to fpin)
Who wrought, and wrought, but, for fome plot,
The caufe of which I've now forgot,

During

During the abfence of the Sun
Undid what She by day had done)
Whilſt they a double viſage wear,
What's ſworn by Day, by Night unſwear.

Such be their Arts, and ſuch perchance
May happily their ends advance :
From a new ſyſtem *mine* ſhall ſpring,
A LOCUM-TENENS is the thing.
That's your true Plan—to obligate
The preſent Miniſters of State,
My *Shadow* ſhall our Court approach,
And bear my pow'r, and have my *coach*,
My *fine State-Coach*, ſuperb to view,
A fine State-Coach, and paid for too ;
To curry favour, and the grace
Obtain, of thoſe who're out of place,
In the mean time *I*—that's to ſay—
I proper, *I* myſelf—*here* ſtay.

But hold—perhaps unto the Nation,
Who hate the Scot's adminiſtration,
To lend my Coach may ſeem to be
Declaring for the Miniſtry,

For

For where the City-Coach is, there
Is the true effence of the MAYOR.
Therefore (for wife men are intent
Evils at diftance to prevent,
Whilft Fools the evils firft endure,
And then are plagu'd to feek a cure)
No *Coach*—a *Horfe*—and free from fear
To make our *Deputy* appear,
Faft on his back fhall he be tied,
With two grooms marching by his fide,
Then for a *Horfe*—thro' all the land,
To head our folemn City-band,
Can any one fo fit be found,
As He, who in *Artill'ry-ground*,
Without a Rider, noble Sight,
Led on our braveft troops to fight.

But firft, CRAPE, for my Honour's fake,
A tender point, enquiry make
About that *Horfe*, if the difpute
Is ended, or is ftill in fuit.
For whilft a caufe (obferve this plan
Of Juftice) whether *Horfe* or *Man*

The

The parties be, remains in doubt,
Till 'tis determin'd out and out,
That Pow'r muſt tyranny appear,
Which ſhould, *Pre-judging*, interfere,
And weak faint Judges over-awe
To bias the free courſe of Law.

You have my will—now quickly run,
And take care that my will be done.
In public, CRAPE, You muſt appear,
Whilſt I in privacy ſit here;
Here ſhall great DULLMAN ſit alone,
Making this Elbow-Chair my throne,
And, You performing what I bid,
Do all, as if I nothing did.

CRAPE heard, and ſpeeded on his way;
With him to hear was to obey;
Not without trouble be aſſur'd,
A proper Proxy was procur'd
To ſerve ſuch infamous intent,
And ſuch a Lord to repreſent,
Nor could one have been found at all
On t'other ſide of *London-wall*.

The

The trumpet founds—folemn and flow
Behold the grand Proceffion go,
All moving on, Cat after kind,
As if for motion ne'er defign'd.

Conftables, whom the Laws admit
To keep the Peace by breaking it ; -
Beadles, who hold the fecond place
By virtue of a filver mace,
Which ev'ry *Saturday* is drawn,
For ufe of *Sunday*, out of pawn ;
Treafurers, who with empty key
Secure an empty Treafury ;
Churchwardens, who their courfe purfue
In the fame ftate, as to their pew
Churchwardens of *Saint Marg'ret* go,
Since PEIRSON taught them pride and fhow,
Who in fhort tranfient pomp appear,
Like Almanacks chang'd ev'ry year,
Behind whom, with unbroken locks,
CHARITY carries the *Poor's Box*,
Not knowing that with private keys
They ope and fhut it when they pleafe,

Overfeers,

Overseers, who by frauds ensure
The heavy curses of the poor;
Unclean came flocking, *Bulls* and *Bears*,
Like Beasts into the ark, by pairs.

Portentous flaming in the van
Stalk'd the *Professor* SHERIDAN;
A Man of *wire*, a mere *Pantine*,
A downright *animal Machine*.
He knows alone in proper mode
How to take vengeance on an *Ode*,
And how to butcher AMMON's Son,
And poor *Jack Dryden* both in One.
On all occasions next the Chair
He stand for service of the MAYOR,
And to instruct him how to use,
His *A*'s and *B*'s, and *P*'s and *Q*'s.
O'er *Letters*, into tatters worn,
O'er *Syllables*, defac'd and torn,
O'er *Words* disjointed, and o'er *Sense*,
Left destitute of all defence,
He strides, and all the way he goes,
Wades, deep in blood, o'er *Crifs-Crofs-Rows*.

Before

Before him ev'ry *Confonant*
In agonies is feen to pant ;
Eehind, in forms not to be known,
The Ghofts of tortur'd *Vowels* groan.

Next HART and DUKE, well worthy grace
And City favour, came in place.
No Children can their toils engage,
Their toils are turn'd to Rev'rend Age,
When a *Court-Dame*, to grace his brows
Refolv'd, is wed to City Spoufe,
Their aid with *Madam*'s aid muft join
The aukward Dotard to refine,
And teach, whence trueft glory flows,
Grave Sixty to turn out his toes.
Each bore in hand a Kit, and each
To fhew how.fit he was to teach
A *Cit*, an *Alderman*, a *Mayor*,
Led in a ftring a *dancing Bear*.

Since the revival of *Fingal*,
Cuftom, and Cuftom's all in all,
Commands that we fhould have regard,
On all high feafons, to the *Bard*.

Great

Great acts like thefe, by vulgar tongue
Profan'd, fhould not be faid, but fung.
This place to fill, renown'd in fame,
The high and mighty LOCKMAN came,
And, ne'er forgot in DULLMAN's reign,
With proper order to maintain
The *Uniformity* of Pride,
Brought *Brother* WHITEHEAD by his fide.

On Horfe, who proudly paw'd the ground,
And caft his fiery eyeballs round,
Snorting, and champing the rude bit,
As if, for warlike purpofe fit,
His high and gen'rous blood difdain'd
To be for fports and paftimes rein'd,
Great DYMOCK, in his glorious ftation,
Paraded at the Coronation.
Not fo our *City* DYMOCK came,
Heavy, difpirited, and tame,
No mark of fenfe, his eyes half-clos'd,
He on a mighty *Dray-horfe* doz'd.
Fate never could a horfe provide
So fit for fuch a man to ride,

Nor find a Man, with ſtricteſt care,

So fit for ſuch a horſe to bear.

Hung round with inſtruments of death,

The ſight of him would ſtop the breath

Of braggart Cowardice, and make

The very *Court Drawcanſir* quake.

With *Durks*, which, in the hands of Spite,

Do their damn'd buſineſs in the Night,

From *Scotland* ſent, but here diſplay'd

Only to fill up the Parade ;

With *Swords*, unfleſh'd, of maiden hue,

Which Rage or Valour never drew ;

With *Blunderbuſſes*, taught to ride,

Like *Pocket-Piſtols*, by his ſide,

In girdle ſtuck, he ſeem'd to be

A little moving *Armory.*

One thing much wanting to complete

The ſight, and make a perfect treat,

Was that the Horſe (a Courteſy

In Horſes found of high degree)

Inſtead of going *forward* on,

All the way *backward* ſhould have gone.

Horſes, unleſs they breeding lack,

Some Scruple make to turn their back,

Tho'

Tho' Riders, which plain Truth declares,
No scruple make of turning theirs.

Far, far apart from all the rest,
Fit only for a standing jest,
The *independent* (can you get
A better suited Epithet)
The *independent* AMYAND came,
All burning with the sacred flame
Of Liberty, which well he knows
On the great stock of slav'ry grows.
Like Sparrow, who, depriv'd of Mate
Snatch'd by the cruel hand of Fate,
From spray to spray no more will hop,
But sits alone on the House-top,
Or like Himself, when all alone
At *Croydon,* he was heard to groan,
Lifting *both* hands in the defence
Of Interest, and Common-Sense;
Both hands, for as no other man
Adopted and pursu'd his plan,
The *Left*-hand had been lonesome quite,
If He had not held up the *right*,

Apart

Apart He came, and fix'd his eyes
With rapture on a diftant prize,
On which in Letters worthy note,
There, TWENTY THOUSAND POUNDS, was wrote.
Falfe trap, for Credit fapp'd is found
By getting twenty thoufand pound;
Nay, look not thus on Me, and ftare,
Doubting the Certainty—to fwear
In fuch a cafe I fhould be loth—
But PERRY CUST may take his oath.

In plain and decent garb array'd,
With the prim Quaker, FRAUD, came TRADE;
CONNIVANCE, to improve the plan,
Habited like a *Jury-man*,
Judging as Intereft prevails,
Came next with meafures, weights, and fcales;
EXTORTION next, of hellifh race,
A Cub moft damn'd, to fhew his face
Forbid by fear, but not by fhame,
Turn'd to a *Jew*, like ——— came;
CORRUPTION, MIDAS-liké, behold
Turning whate'er She touch'd to gold,

IMPOTENCE led by LUST, and PRIDE
Strutting with PONTON by her side,
HYPOCRISY, demure and sad,
In garments of the Priesthood clad,
So well disguis'd, that You might swear,
Deceiv'd, a very Priest was there ;
BANKRUPTCY, full of ease and health,
And wallowing in *well-sav'd* wealth,
Came sneering thro' a ruin'd band,
And bringing B——— in her hand ;
VICTORY, hanging down her head,
Was by a highland Stallion led ;
PEACE, cloath'd in sables, with a face
Which witness'd sense of huge disgrace,
Which spake a deep and rooted shame
Both of Herself and of her Name,
Mourning creeps on, and blushing feels
WAR, grim WAR treading on her heels ;
Pale CREDIT, shaken by the arts
Of men with bad heads and worse hearts,
Taking no notice of a band
Which near her were ordain'd to stand,
Well nigh destroy'd by sickly fit,
Look'd wistful all around for PITT.

FREEDOM

FREEDOM—at that moſt hallow'd name
My Spirits mount into a flame,
Each pulſe beats high, and each nerve ſtrains
E'en to the cracking; thro' my veins
The tides of life more rapid run,
And tell me I am FREEDOM's Son—
FREEDOM came next, but ſcarce was ſeen,
When the ſky, which appear'd ſerene
And gay before, was overcaſt;
Horror beſtrode a *foreign* blaſt,
And from the *priſon* of the *North*,
To FREEDOM deadly, Storms burſt forth.

A *Car* like thoſe, in which, we're told,
Our wild Forefathers warr'd of old,
Loaded with Death, ſix Horſes bear
Thro' the blank region of the air.
Too fierce for time or art to tame,
They pour'd forth mingled ſmoke and flame
From their wide Noſtrils; ev'ry Steed
Was of that ancient ſavage breed
Which fell GERYON nurs'd; their food
The fleſh of Man, their drink his blood.

On

On the firft Horfes, ill-match'd pair,
This fat and fleek, *That* lean and bare,
Came ill-match'd Riders fide by fide,
And POVERTY was yok'd with PRIDE.
Union moft ftrange it muft appear,
Till other Unions make it clear.

Next, in the gall of bitternefs,
With rage, which words can ill exprefs,
With unforgiving rage, which fprings
From a falfe zeal for holy things,
Wearing fuch robes as Prophets wear,
Falfe Prophets plac'd in PETER's chair,
On which, in Characters of fire,
Shapes Antic, horrible and dire,
Inwoven flam'd, where, to the view,
In groups appear'd a rabble crew
Of Sainted Devils, where all round
Vile *Reliques* of vile men were found,
Who, worfe than Devils, from the birth
Perform'd the work of Hell on earth,
Jugglers, *Inquifitors*, and *Popes*,
Pointing at *axes*, *wheels*, and *ropes*,

K 4 And

And *Engines*, fram'd on horrid plan,
Which none but the deftroyer, Man,
Could, to promote his felfifh views,
Have heads to make, or hearts to ufe,
Bearing, to confecrate her tricks,
In her left-hand a *Crucifix*,
Remembrance of Our dying Lord,
And in her right a *two-edg'd fword*;
Having her brows, in impious fport,
Adorn'd with words of high import,
On earth PEACE, *amongft men*, GOOD WILL,
LOVE *bearing*, and *forbearing* ftill,
All wrote in the *hearts-blood* of thofe
Who rather Death than Falfhood chofe;
On her breaft, (where, in days of Yore,
When God lov'd *Jews*, the HIGH-PRIEST wore
Thofe Oracles, which were decreed
T' inftruct and guide the chofen feed)
Having with glory clad and ftrength,
The VIRGIN pictur'd at *full length*,
Whilft at her feet, in *fmall* pourtray'd,
As fcarce worth notice, CHRIST was·laid,
Came SUPERSTITION, fierce and fell,
An Imp detefted, e'en in hell;

                                    Her

Her Eye inflam'd, her face all o'er
Foully befmear'd with human gore,
O'er heaps of mangled *Saints* She rode ;
Faft at her heels DEATH proudly ftrode,
And grimly fmil'd, well-pleas'd to fee
Such havock of mortality.
Clofe by her fide, on mifchief bent,
And urging on each bad intent
To its full bearing, Savage, Wild,
The Mother fit of fuch a child,
Striving the empire to advance
Of Sin and Death, came IGNORANCE.

With looks, where dread command was plac'd,
And Sov'reign Pow'r by Pride difgrac'd,
Where, loudly witneffing a mind
Of favage more than human kind,
Not chufing to be lov'd, but fear'd,
Mocking at right, MISRULE appear'd,
With Eyeballs glaring fiery red
Enough to ftrike beholders dead,
Gnafhing his teeth, and in a flood
Pouring corruption forth and blood

From

From his chaf'd jaws; without remorfe
Whipping, and fpurring on his horfe,
Wnofe fides, in their own blood embay'd,
E'en to the bone were open laid,
Came TYRANNY; difdaining awe,
And trampling over *Senfe* and *Law.*
One thing and only one He knew,
One object only would purfue,
Tho' Lefs (fo low doth paffion bring)
Than man, he would be more than King.

With ev'ry argument and art,
Which might corrupt the head and heart,
Soothing the frenzy of his mind,
Companion meet, was FLATT'RY join'd.
Winning his carriage, ev'ry look
Employ'd, whilft it conceal'd a hook;
When fimple moft, moft to be fear'd;
Moft crafty, when no craft appear'd;
His tales, no man like him could tell;
His words, which melted as they fell,
Might e'en a Hypocrite deceive,
And make an infidel believe,

Wantonly

Wantonly cheating o'er and o'er
Thofe who had cheated been before,
Such FLATT'RY came in evil hour,
Pois'ning the royal ear of pow'r,
And, grown by *Proftitution* great,
Would be firft Minifter of State.

Within the Chariot, all alone,
High feated on a kind of throne,
With pebbles grac'd, a Figure came,
Whom Juftice would, but dare not, name.
Hard times when Juftice, without fear,
Dare not bring forth to public ear
The names of thofe, who dare offend
'Gainft Juftice, and pervert her end;
But, if the Mufe afford me grace,
Defcription fhall fupply the place.

In *foreign* garments he was clad,
Sage Ermine o'er the gloffy *Plaid*,
Caft rev'rend honour, on his heart,
Wrought by the curious hand of Art,
In filver wrought, and brighter far
Than heav'nly or than earthly Star,

Shone

Shone a *White Rose*, the Emblem dear
Of him He ever muft revere,
Of that dread Lord, who, with hĭs hoft
Of faithful native rebels loft,
Like thofe black Spirits doom'd to hell,
At once from pow'r and virtue fell ;
Around his clouded brows was plac'd
A *Bonnet*, moft fuperbly grac'd
With mighty *Thiftles*, nor forgot
The facred motto, *Touch me not.*

In the right-hand a fword He bore
Harder than Adamant, and more
Fatal than winds, which from the mouth
Of the rough North invade the South ;
The reeking blade to view prefents
The blood of helplefs Innocents,
And on the hilt, as meek become
As Lambs before the Shearers dumb,
With downcaft eye, and folemn fhow,
Of deep unutterable woe,
Mourning the time when FREEDOM reign'd,
Faft to a rock was Juftice chain'd.

In

In his left hand, in wax impreſt,
With bells and gewgaws idly dreſt,
An *Image*, caſt in baby mould,
He held, and feem'd o'erjoy'd to hold.
On this he fix'd his eyes, to this
Bowing he gave the loyal kiſs,
And, for Rebellion fully ripe,
Seem'd to deſire the ANTITYPE.
What if to that *Pretender*'s foes
His greatneſs, nay, his life he owes,
Shall common obligations bind,
And ſhake his conſtancy of mind?
Scorning ſuch weak and petty chains,
Faithful to JAMES he ſtill remains,
Tho' he the friend of GEORGE appear:
Diſſimulation's Virtue here.

Jealous and Mean, he with a frown
Would awe, and keep all merit down,
Nor would to Truth and Juſtice bend,
Unleſs *out-bullied* by his *friend*;
Brave with the Coward, with the brave
He is himſelf a Coward ſlave;

Aw'd

Aw'd by his fears, he has no heart
To take a great and open part;
Mines in a fubtle train he fprings,
And, fecret, faps the ears of Kings;
But not e'en there continues firm
'Gainft the refiftance of a worm;
Born in a Country, *where the will*
Of One is Law to all, he ftill
Retain'd th' infection, with full aim
To fpread it wherefoe'er he came;
Freedom he hated, *Law* defied,
The Proftitute of Pow'r and Pride;
Law he with eafe explains away,
And leads bewilder'd Senfe aftray;
Much to the credit of his brain
Puzzles the caufe he can't maintain,
Proceeds on moft familiar grounds,
And, where he can't convince, confounds;
Talents of rareft ftamp and fize,
To Nature falfe, he mifapplies,
And turns to poifon what was fent
For purpofes of nourifhment.

Palenefs,

THE GHOST.

Palenefs, not fuch as on his wings
The Meffenger of Sicknefs brings,
But fuch as takes its coward rife
From confcious bafenefs, confcious vice,
O'erfpread his cheeks ; *Difdain* and *Pride,*
To upftart Fortunes ever tied,
Scowl'd on his brow ; within his eye,
Infidious, lurking like a fpy
To Caution principled by Fear,
Not daring open to appear,
Lodg'd covert *Mifchief* ; *Paffion* hung
On his lip quiv'ring ; on his tongue
Fraud dwelt at large ; within his breaft
All that makes Villain found a neft,
All that, on hell's compleateft plan,
E'er join'd to damn the heart of man.

Soon as the Car reach'd land, He rofe,
And with a look which might have froze
The heart's beft blood, which was enough
Had hearts been made of fterner ftuff
In Cities than elfewhere, to make
The very ftouteft quail and quake,

He caft his baleful eyes around ;
Fix'd without motion to the ground,
Fear waiting on furprize, All ftood,
And Horror chill'd their curdled blood,
No more they thought of *Pomp*, no more
(For they had feen his face before)
Of *Law* they thought ; the caufe forgot,
Whether it was or Ghoft, or Plot,
Which drew them there. They all ftood more
Like Statues than they were before.

What could be done ? Could Art, could Force,
Or Both direct a proper courfe
To make this favage Monfter tame,
Or fend him back the way he came ?
What neither Art, nor Force, nor Both
Could do, a *Lord* of foreign growth,
A Lord to that bafe wretch allied
In Country, not in Vice and Pride,
Effected ; from the felf-fame land,
(Bad news for our blafpheming band
Of Scribblers, but deferving note)
The Poifon came, and Antidote.

Abafh'd

'Abafh'd the Monfter hung his head;
And, like an empty Vifion, fled;
His Train, like Virgin Snows which run,
Kifs'd by the burning bawdy Sun,
To lovefick ftreams, diffolv'd in Air;
Joy, who from abfence feem'd more fair,
Came fmiling, freed from flavifh awe;
LOYALTY, LIBERTY, and LAW,
Impatient of the galling chain,
And Yoke of pow'r, refum'd their reign;
And, burning with the glorious flame
Of Public Virtue, MANSFIELD came.

END OF THE GHOST.

THE

ONFERENCE.

L 2

THE

CONFERENCE.

G RACE faid in form, which Sceptics muſt agree,
When they are told that Grace was faid by Me;
The Servants gone, to break the ſcurvy jeſt
On the proud Landlord, and his thread-bare gueſt;
The King gone round, my Lady too withdrawn,
My Lord, in uſual taſte, began to yawn,
And lolling backward in his elbow-chair,
With an inſipid kind of ſtupid ſtare,

Picking

Picking his teeth, twirling his feals about—
CHURCHILL, You have a Poem coming out.
You've my beft wifhes ; but I really fear
Your Mufe in general is too fevere,
Her Spirit feems her int'reft to oppofe,
And where fhe makes one friend, makes twenty foes.

C. Your Lordfhip's fears are juft, I feel their force,
But only feel it as a thing of courfe.
The man whofe hardy fpirit fhall engage
To lafh the vices of a guilty age,
At his firft fetting forward ought to know,
That ev'ry rogue he meets muft be his foe,
That the rude breath of Satire will provoke
Many who feel, and more who fear the ftroke.
But fhall the partial rage of felfifh men
From ftubborn juftice wrench the righteous pen,
Or fhall I not my fettled courfe purfue,
Becaufe my foes, are foes to Virtue too ?

L. What is this boafted Virtue, taught in fchools,
And idly drawn from antiquated rules ?
What is her ufe ? point out one wholefome end ?
Will fhe hurt foes, or can fhe make a friend ?

When

When from long fasts fierce appetites arise,
Can this same Virtue stifle Nature's cries?
Can she the pittance of a meal afford,
Or bid thee welcome to one great man's board?
When northern winds the rough December arm
With frost and snow, can Virtue keep thee warm?
Canst thou dismiss the hard unfeeling Dun
Barely by saying, Thou art Virtue's Son?
Or by base blundring Statesmen sent to jail,
Will MANSFIELD take this Virtue for thy bail?
Believe it not, the name is in disgrace,
Virtue and TEMPLE now are out of place.

Quit then this meteor, whose delusive ray
From wealth and honour leads thee far astray.
True Virtue means, let Reason use her eyes,
Nothing with Fools, and Int'rest with the Wise.
Would'st thou be great, her patronage disclaim,
Nor madly triumph in so mean a name:
Let nobler wreaths thy happy brows adorn,
And leave to Virtue poverty and scorn.
Let Prudence be thy guide; who doth not know
How seldom Prudence can with Virtue go?

To

To be fuccefsful try thy utmoft force,
And Virtue follows as a thing of courfe.

HIRCO, who knows not HIRCO, ftains the bed
Of that kind Mafter who firft gave him bread,
Scatters the feeds of difcord thro' the land,
Breaks ev'ry public, ev'ry private band,
Beholds with joy a trufting friend undone,
Betrays a Brother, and would cheat a Son :
What mortal in his fenfes can endure
The name of HIRCO, for the wretch is poor !
" Let him hang, drown, ftarve, on a dunghill rot,
" By all detefted live, and die forgot ;
" Let him, a poor return, in ev'ry breath
" Feel all death's pains, yet be whole years in death,"
Is now the gen'ral cry we all purfue ;
Let FORTUNE change, and PRUDENCE changes too,
Supple and pliant a new fyftem feels,
Throws up her Cap, and fpaniels at his heels,
Long live great HIRCO, cries, by int'reft taught,
And let his foes, tho' I prove one, be nought.

C. Peace to fuch Men, if fuch Men can have peace,
Let their Poffeffions, let their State increafe,

Let

Let their bafe fervices in Courts ftrike root,
. And in the feafon bring forth golden fruit,
I envy not ; let thofe who have the will,
And, with fo little Spirit, fo much fkill,
With fuch vile inftruments their fortunes carve ;
Rogues may grow fat, an honeft man dares ftarve.

L. Thefe ftale conceits thrown off, let us advance
For once to real life, and quit Romance.
Starve! pretty talking! but I fain would view
That man, that honeft man, would do it too.
Hence to yon mountain which outbraves the fky,
And dart from pole to pole thy ftrengthen'd eye,
Thro' all that fpace you fhall not view one man,
Not one, who dares to act on fuch a plan.
Cowards in calms will fay, what in a ftorm,
The Brave will tremble at, and not perform.
Thine be the proof, and, fpite of all you've faid,
You'd give your Honour for a cruft of bread.

C. What Proof might do, what Hunger might effect,
What famifh'd Nature, looking with neglect
On all fhe once held dear, what Fear, at ftrife
With fainting Virtue for the means of life,

Might

Might make this coward flesh, in love with breath,
Shudd'ring at pain, and shrinking back from death,
In treason to my foul, descend to bear,
Trusting to Fate, I neither know nor care.

Once, at this hour those wounds afresh I feel,
Which nor prosperity nor time can heal,
Those wounds, which Fate severely hath decreed,
Mention'd or thought of, must for ever bleed,
Those wounds, which humbled all that pride of man,
Which brings such mighty aid to Virtue's plan;
Once, aw'd by Fortune's most oppressive frown,
By legal rapine to the earth bow'd down,
My credit at last gasp, my state undone,
Trembling to meet the shock I could not shun,
Virtue gave ground, and black despair prevail'd;
Sinking beneath the storm, my spirits fail'd,
Like PETER's Faith, 'till One, a Friend indeed,
May all distress find such in time of need,
One kind good man, in act, in word, in thought,
By Virtue guided, and by Wisdom taught,
Image of him whom Christians should adore,
Stretch'd forth his hand, and brought me safe to shore.

Since,

Since, by good fortune into notice rais'd,
And for some little merit largely prais'd,
Indulg'd in swerving from prudential rules,
Hated by rogues, and not belov'd by fools,
Plac'd above want, shall abject thirst of wealth
So fiercely war 'gainst my soul's dearest health,
That, as a boon, I should base shackles crave,
And, born to freedom, make myself a slave ;
That I should in the train of those appear,
Whom Honour cannot love, nor Manhood fear ?

That I no longer skulk from street to street,
Afraid left Duns assail, and Bailiffs meet ;
That I from place to place this carcase bear,
Walk forth at large, and wander free as air ;
That I no longer dread the aukward friend,
Whose very obligations must offend,
Nor, all too forward, with impatience burn
At suff'ring favours which I can't return ;
That, from dependance and from pride secure,
I am not plac'd so high to scorn the poor,
Nor yet so low, that I my Lord should fear,
Or hesitate to give him sneer for sneer ;

That

That, whilft fage Prudence my purfuits confirms,
I can enjoy the world on equal terms ;
That, kind to others, to myfelf moft true,
Feeling no want, I comfort thofe who do,
And with the will have power to aid diftrefs ;
Thefe, and what other bleffings I poffefs,
From the indulgence of the PUBLIC rife ;
All private patronage my foul defies.
By Candour more inclin'd to fave, than damn,
A gen'rous PUBLIC made me what I Am.
All that I have, They gave ; juft mem'ry bears
The grateful ftamp, and what I am is Theirs.

L. To feign a red-hot zeal for Freedom's caufe,
To mouth aloud for liberties and laws,
For public good to bellow all abroad,
Serves well the purpofes of private fraud.
Prudence, by public good intends her own ;
If you mean otherwife, you ftand alone.
What do we mean by Country and by Court,
What is it to Oppofe, what to Support ?
Mere words of courfe, and what is more abfurd
Than to pay homage to an empty word !

MAJORS

MAJORS and MINORS differ but in name,
Patriots and Minifters are much the fame;
The only diff'rence, after all their rout,
Is that the One is *in*, the Other *out*.

Explore the dark receffes of the mind,
In the Soul's honeft volume read mankind,
And own, in wife and fimple, great and fmall,
The fame grand leading Principle in All.
Whate'er we talk of wifdom to the wife,
Of goodnefs to the good, of public ties
Which to our country link, of private bands
Which claim moft dear attention at our hands,
For Parent and for Child, for Wife and Friend,
Our firft great Mover, and our laft great End,
Is One, and, by whatever name we call
The ruling Tyrant SELF is All in All.
This, which unwilling Faction fhall admit,
Guided in diff'rent ways a BUTE and PITT,
Made Tyrants break, made Kings obferve the law,
And gave the world a STUART and NASSAU.

Hath Nature (ftrange and wild conceit of Pride)
Diftinguifh'd thee from all her fons befide?

Doth

Doth Virtue in thy bofom brighter glow,
Or from a fpring more pure doth Action flow?
Is not thy foul bound with thofe very chains
Which fhackle us, or is that SELF, which reigns
O'er Kings and Beggars, which in all we fee
Moft ftrong and fov'reign, only weak in Thee?
Fond man, believe it not; experience tells
'Tis not thy Virtue, but thy Pride rebels.
Think (and for once lay by thy lawlefs pen)
Think, and confefs thyfelf like other men;
Think but one hour, and, to thy Confcience led
By Reafon's hand, bow down and hang thy head;
Think on thy private life, recal thy youth,
View thyfelf now, and own with ftricteft truth,
That SELF hath drawn thee from fair Virtue's way
Farther than Folly would have dar'd to ftray,
And that the talents lib'ral Nature gave
To make thee free, have made thee more a flave.

Quit then, in prudence quit, that idle train
Of toys, which have fo long abus'd thy brain,
And captive led thy pow'rs; with boundlefs will
Let SELF maintain her ftate and empire ftill,

But

But let her, with more worthy objects caught,
Strain all the faculties and force of thought
To things of higher daring ; let her range
Thro' better pastures, and learn how to change ;
Let her, no longer to weak faction tied,
Wisely revolt, and join our stronger side.

C. Ah! what, my Lord, hath private life to do
With things of public nature ? why to view
Would you thus cruelly those scenes unfold,
Which, without pain and horror to behold,
Must speak me something more, or less than man ;
Which Friends may pardon, but I never can ?
Look back! a thought which borders on despair,
Which human nature must, yet cannot bear.
'Tis not the babbling of a busy world,
Where praise and censure are at random hurl'd,
Which can the meanest of my thoughts controul,
Or shake one settled purpose of my soul.
Free and at large might their wild curses roam,
If All, if All alas! were well at home.
No—'tis the tale which angry Conscience tells,
When she with more than tragic horror swells

Each

Each circumftance of guilt; when ftern, but true,
She brings bad actions forth into review ;
And, like the dread hand-writing on the wall,
Bids late Remorfe awake at Reafon's call,
Arm'd at all points bids Scorpion Vengeance pafs,
And to the mind holds up Reflection's glafs,
The mind, which ftarting, heaves the heart-felt groan,
And hates that form fhe knows to be her own.

Enough of this—let private forrows reft—
As to the Public I dare ftand the teft ;
Dare proudly boaft, I feel no wifh above
The good of ENGLAND, and my Country's love.
Stranger to party-rage, by Reafon's voice,
Uncrring guide, directed in my choice,
Not all the tyrant pow'rs of earth combin'd,
No, nor of hell, fhall make me change my mind.
What! herd with men my honeft foul difdains,
Men who, with fervile zeal, are forging chains
For Freedom's neck, and lend a helping hand,
To fpread deftruction o'er my native land.
What! fhall I not, e'en to my lateft breath,
In the full face of danger and of death,

Exert

Exert that little ſtrength which Nature gave,
And boldly ſtem, or periſh in the wave?

L. When I look backward for ſome fifty years,
And ſee *Proteſting* Patriots turn'd to Peers ;
Hear men, moſt looſe, for decency declaim,
And talk of Character without a name ;
See Infidels aſſert the cauſe of God,
And meek Divines wield Perſecution's rod ;
See men transform'd to brutes, and brutes to men,
See WHITEHEAD take a place, Ralph change his pen,
I mock the zeal, and deem the men in ſport,
Who rail at Miniſters, and curſe a Court.
Thee, haughty as thou art, and proud in rime,
Shall ſome Preferment, offer'd at a time
When Virtue ſleeps, ſome Sacrifice to Pride,
Or ſome fair Victim, move to change thy ſide.
Thee ſhall theſe eyes behold, to health reſtor'd,
Uſing, as Prudence bids, bold Satire's ſword,
Galling thy preſent friends, and praiſing thoſe,
Whom now thy frenzy holds thy greateſt foes.

C. May I, (can worſe diſgrace on manhood fall ?)
De born a WHITEHEAD, and baptiz'd a PAUL ;

May I (tho' to his fervice deeply tied
By facred oaths, and now by will allied)
With falfe feign'd zeal an injur'd God defend,
And ufe his name for fome bafe private end ;
May I (that thought bids double horrors roll
O'er my fick fpirits, and unmans my foul)
Ruin the Virtue which I held moft dear,
And ftill muft hold ; may I, thro' abjeft fear,
Betray my friend ; may to fucceeding times,
Engrav'd on plates of adamant, my crimes
Stand blazing forth, whilft mark'd with envious blot,
Each little act of Virtue is forgot ;
Of all thofe evils which, to ftamp men curs'd,
Hell keeps in, ftore for vengeance, may the worft
Light on my head, and in my day of woe,
To make the cup of bitternefs o'erflow,
May I be fcorn'd by ev'ry man of worth,
Wander, like Cain, a vagabond on earth,
Bearing about a hell in my own mind,
Or be to SCOTLAND for my life confin'd,
If I am one among the many known,
Whom SHELBURNE fled, and CALCRAFT blufh'd to own.

L. Do

L. Do you reflect what men you make your foes?

C. I do, and that's the reason I oppose;
Friends I have made, whom Envy muft commend,
But not one foe, whom I would wifh a friend.
What if ten thoufand BUTES and HOLLANDS bawl,
One WILKES hath made a large amends for all.

'Tis not the Title, whether handed down
From age to age, or flowing from the crown
In copious ftreams on recent men, who came
From ftems unknown, and fires without a name;
'Tis not the *Star*, which our great EDWARD gave
To mark the virtuous, and reward the brave,
Blazing without, whilft a bafe heart within
Is rotten to the core with filth and fin;
'Tis not the tinfel grandeur, taught to wait,
At cuftom's call, to mark a fool of State
From fools of leffer note, that Soul can awe
Whofe Pride is Reafon, whofe Defence is Law.

L. Suppofe (a thing fcarce poffible in Art,
Were it thy Cue to play a common Part;)

Suppof

Suppofe thy Writings fo well fenc'd in Law,

That N— — cannot find, nor make a Flaw,

Haft thou not heard, that 'mongft our ancient Tribes,

By Party warpt, or lull'd afleep by Bribes,

Or trembling at the Ruffian Hand of Force,

Law hath fufpended ftood, or chang'd its Courfe?

Art thou affur'd, that, for Deftruction ripe,

Thou may'ft not fmart beneath the felf-fame Gripe?

What Sanction haft thou, frantic in thy Rimes,

Thy Life, thy Freedom to fecure?

C. The Times.

'Tis not on Law, a Syftem great and good,

By Wifdom penn'd, and bought by nobleft Blood,

My Faith relies : By wicked Men and vain,

Law, once abus'd, may be abus'd again.—

No, on our great Law-giver I depend,

Who knows and guides her to her proper End;

Whofe Royalty of Nature blazes out

So fierce, 'twere Sin to entertain a doubt—

Did Tyrant STUARTS now the Laws difpenfe,

(Bleft be the hour and hand which fent them hence)

For fomething, or for nothing, for a word,

Or thought, I might be doom'd to Death, *unheard.*

Life

Life we might all refign to lawlefs Pow'r,
Nor think it worth the purchafe of an hour;
But Envy ne'er fhall fix fo foul a ftain
On the fair annals of a BRUNSWICK's reign.

If, Slave to Party, to Revenge, or Pride,
If, by frail human Error drawn afide,
I break the Law, ftrict rigour let her wear;
'Tis her's to punifh, and 'tis mine to bear;
Nor, by the voice of Juftice doom'd to death,
Would I afk mercy with my lateft breath.
But, anxious only for my Country's good,
In which my King's, *of courfe*, is underftood;
Form'd on a plan with fome few Patriot friends,
Whilft by juft means I aim at nobleft ends,
My Spirits cannot fink; tho' from the tomb
Stern JEFFRIES fhould be plac'd in MANSFIELD's room,
Tho' he fhould bring, his bafe defigns to aid,
Some *black Attorney*, for his purpofe made,
And fhove, whilft Decency and Law retreat,
The modeft NORTON from his Maiden feat,
Tho' both, in ill Confed'rates, fhould agree,
In damned league, to torture Law and me,

Whilft

Whilſt GEORGE is King, I cannot fear endure;
Not to be guilty, is to be ſecure.

Eut when, in after-times, (be far remov'd
That day) our Monarch, glorious and belov'd,
Sleeps with his Fathers, ſhould imperious Fate,
In vengeance, with freſh STUARTS curſe our ſtate;
Should they, o'erleaping ev'ry fence of Law,
Butcher the brave to keep tame fools in awe;
Should they, by brutal and oppreſſive force,
Divert ſweet Juſtice from her even courſe;
Should they, of ev'ry other means bereft,
Make my right-hand a witneſs 'gainſt my left;
Should they, abroad by Inquiſitions taught,
Search out my Soul, and damn me for a thought,
Still would I keep my courſe, ſtill ſpeak, ſtill write,
'Till Death had plung'd me in the ſhades of Night.

Thou GOD of *Truth*, thou great, all-ſearching Eye,
To whom our Thoughts, our Spirits open lie,
Grant me thy ſtrength, and in that needful hour,
(Should it e'er come) when Law ſubmits to Pow'r,
With firm reſolve my ſteady boſom ſteel,
Bravely to ſuffer, tho' I deeply feel.

                                                    Let

Let me, as hitherto, ſtill draw my breath,
In love with life, but not in fear of death,
And, if Oppreſſion brings me to the grave,
And marks me dead, ſhe ne'er ſhall mark a ſlave,
Let no unworthy marks of grief be heard,
No wild laments, not one unſeemly word;
Let ſober Triumphs wait upon my bier,
I won't forgive that friend who drops one tear.
Whether he's raviſh'd in life's early morn,
Or, in old age, drops like an ear of Corn,
Full ripe he falls, on Nature's nobleſt plan,
Who lives to Reaſon, and who dies a Man.

THE END.

THE

THE

AUTHOR.

T H E

H T U

THE

AUTHOR.

ACCURS'D the man, whom fate ordains in spite,
And cruel parents teach, to Read and Write!
What need of letters? Wherefore should we spell?
Why write our names? A mark will do as well.

Much are the precious hours of youth mispent,
In climbing Learning's rugged steep ascent;
When to the top the bold advent'rer's got,
He reigns, vain monarch, o'er a barren spot,

Whilst

Whilft in the *vale* of *Ignorance* below,
FOLLY and VICE to rank luxuriance grow ;
Honours and wealth pour in on ev'ry fide,
And proud preferment rolls her golden tide.

O'er crabbed authors life's gay prime to wafte,
To cramp wild genius in the chains of tafte,
To bear the flavifh drudgery of fchools,
And tamely ftoop to ev'ry pedant's rules,
For feven long years debarr'd of lib'ral eafe,
To plod in college trammels to *degrees*,
Beneath the weight of folemn toys to groan,
Sleep over books, and leave mankind unknown,
To praife each fenior blockhead's thread-bare tale,
And laugh till reafon blufh, and fpirits fail,
Manhood with vile fubmiffion to difgrace,
And *cap* the fool, whofe merit is his Place ;
VICE CHANCELLORS, whofe knowledge is but fmall,
And CHANCELLORS, who nothing know at all,
Ill-brook'd the gen'rous Spirit in thofe days
When Learning was the certain road to praife,
When Nobles, with a love of Science blefs'd,
Approv'd in others what themfelves poffefs'd.

                                                    But

But *Now*, when DULLNESS rears aloft her throne,
When LORDLY Vaffals her wide Empire own,
When Wit, feduc'd by Envy, ftarts afide,
And bafely leagues with Ignorance and Pride,
What *Now* fhould tempt us, by falfe hopes mifled,
Learning's unfafhionable paths to tread;
To bear thofe labours, which our Fathers bore,
That Crown with-held, which they in triumph wore?

When with much pains this boafted Learning's got,
'Tis an affront to thofe who have it not.
In fome it caufes hate, in others fear,
Inftructs our foes to rail, our friends to fneer.
With prudent hafte the worldly-minded fool,
Forgets the little which he learn'd at School;
The Elder Brother, to vaft fortunes born,
Looks on all Science with an Eye of Scorn;
Dependent Brethren the fame features wear,
And younger Sons are ftupid as the Heir.
In Senates, at the Bar, in Church and State,
Genius is vile, and Learning out of date.

Is this—O Death to think! is this the Land
Where Merit and Reward went hand in hand,

Where

Where Heroes, Parent-like, the Poet view'd,

By whom they faw their glorious deeds renew'd ;

Where Poets, true to Honour, tun'd their lays,

And by their Patrons fanctify'd their praife ?

Is this the Land, where, on our SPENCER's tongue,

Enamour'd of his voice, Defcription hung ;

Where JONSON rigid gravity beguil'd,

Whilft Reafon thro' her Critic fences fmil'd ;

WhereNATURElift'ningftood,whilftSHAKESPEARplay'd,

And wonder'd at the Work herfelf had made ?

Is this the Land, where, mindful of her charge

And office high, fair Freedom walk'd at large ;

Where, finding in our Laws a fure defence,

She mock'd at all reftraints, but thofe of Senfe ;

Where health and honour trooping by her fide,

She fpread her facred empire far and wide ;

Pointed the way, Affliction to beguile,

And bade the face of Sorrow wear a fmile,

Bade thofe, who dare obey the gen'rous call,

Enjoy her bleffings, which GOD meant for all ?

Is this the Land, where in fome Tyrant's reign,

When a *weak, wicked, Minifterial* train,

The tools of pow'r, the flaves of int'reft, plann'd

Their Country's ruin, and with bribes unman'd

Thofe

Those wretches, who, ordain'd in Freedom's cause,
Gave up our liberties, and sold our laws;
When Pow'r was taught by Meanness where to go,
Nor dar'd to love the Virtue of a foe;
When, like a lep'rous plague, from the foul head
To the foul heart her sores Corruption spread,
Her iron arm when stern Oppression rear'd,
And Virtue, from her broad base shaken, fear'd
The scourge of Vice; when, impotent and vain,
Poor Freedom bow'd the neck to Slav'ry's chain;
Is this the Land, where in those worst of times,
The hardy Poet rais'd his honest rimes
To dread rebuke, and bade controulment speak
In guilty blushes on the villain's cheek,
Bade Pow'r turn pale, kept mighty rogues in awe,
And made them fear the Muse, who fear'd not Law?

How do I laugh, when men of narrow souls,
Whom folly guides, and prejudice controuls;
Who, one dull drowsy track of business trod,
Worship their Mammon, and neglect their God;
Who, breathing by one musty set of rules,
Dote from the birth, and are by system fools;

Who,

Who, form'd to dullnefs from their very youth,
Lies of the day prefer to Gofpel truth,
Pick up their little knowledge from Reviews,
And lay out all their ftock of faith in news :
How do I laugh, when Creatures, form'd like thefe,
Whom Reafon fcorns, and I fhould blufh to pleafe,
Rail at all lib'ral arts, deem verfe a crime,
And hold not Truth, as Truth, if told in rime ?

How do I laugh, when Publius, hoary groan
In zeal for Scotland's welfare, and his own,
By flow degrees, and courfe of office, drawn
In mood and figure at the helm to yawn,
Too mean (the worft of curfes Heav'n can fend)
To have a foe, too proud to have a friend,
Erring by form, which Blockheads facred hold,
Ne'er making new faults, and ne'er mending old,
Rebukes my Spirit, bids the daring Mufe
Subjects more equal to her weaknefs chufe;
Bids her frequent the haunts of humble fwains,
Nor dare to traffick in ambitious ftrains;
Bids her, indulging the poetic whim
In quaint-wrought Ode, or Sonnet pertly trim,

Along the Church-way path complain with GRAY,
Or dance with MASON on the firft of May?
" All facred is the name and pow'r of Kings,
" All States and Statefmen are thofe mighty Things
" Which, howfoe'er they out of courfe may roll,
" Were never made for Poets to controul."

Peace, Peace thou Dotard, nor thus vilely deem
Of Sacred Numbers, and their pow'r blafpheme;
I tell thee, Wretch, fearch all creation round,
In Earth, in Heav'n, no Subject can be found
(Our God alone except) above whofe weight
The Poet cannot rife, and hold his State.
The bleffed Saints above in numbers fpeak
The praife of God, tho' there all praife is weak;
In Numbers here below the Bard fhall teach
Virtue to foar beyond the Villain's reach;
Shall tear his lab'ring lungs, ftrain his hoarfe throat,
And raife his voice beyond the trumpet's note,
Should an afflicted Country, aw'd by men
Of flavifh principles, demand his pen.
This is a great, a glorious point of view,
Fit for an Englifh Poet to purfue,

Undaunted to purfue, tho', in return,
His writings by the common Hangman burn.

How do I laugh, when men, by fortune plac'd
Above their Betters, and by rank difgrac'd,
Who found their pride on titles which they ftain,
And, mean themfelves, are of their Fathers vain,
Who would a bill of privilege prefer,
And treat a Poet like a Creditor,
The gen'rous ardor of the Mufe condemn,
And curfe the ftorm they know muft break on them.
" What, fhall a reptile Bard, a wretch unknown,
" Without one badge of merit, but his own,
" Great Nobles lafh, and *Lords*, like common men,
" Smart from the vengeance of a Scribbler's pen?"

What's in this name of *Lord*, that I fhould fear
To bring their vices to the public ear?
Flows not the honeft blood of humble fwains
Quick as the tide which fwells a Monarch's veins?
Monarchs, who wealth and titles can beftow,
Cannot make Virtues in fucceffion flow.
Would'ft thou, proud Man, be fafely plac'd above
The cenfure of the Mufe, deferve her love,

Act

Act as thy Birth demands, as Nobles ought;
Look back, and by thy worthy Father taught,
Who *earn'd* thofe Honours, thou wert *lorn* to wear,
Follow his fteps, and be his Virtue's heir.
But if, regardlefs of the road to Fame,
You ftart afide, and tread the paths of Shame,
If fuch thy life, that fhould thy Sire arife,
The fight of fuch a Son would blaft his eyes,
Would make him curfe the hour which gave thee birth,
Would drive him, fhudd'ring, from the face of earth
Once more, with fhame and forrow, 'mongft the dead
In endlefs night to hide his rev'rend head;
If fuch thy life, tho' Kings had made thee more
Than ever King a fcoundrel made before,
Nay, to allow thy pride a deeper fpring,
Tho' God in vengeance had made thee a King,
Taking on Virtue's wing her daring flight,
The Mufe fhould drag thee trembling to the light,
Probe thy foul wounds, and lay thy bofom bare
To the keen queftion of the fearching air.

Gods! with what pride I fee the titled flave,
Who fmarts beneath the ftroke which Satire gave,

Aiming

Aiming at eafe, and with difhoneſt art,

Striving to hide the feelings of his heart !

How do I laugh, when with affected air,

(Scarce able thro' defpite to keep his chair,

Whilſt on his trembling lip pale anger ſpeaks,

And the chaf'd blood flies mounting to his cheeks}

He talks of Confcience, which good men fecures

From all thofe evil moments guilt endures,

And feems to laugh at thofe, who pay regard

To the wild ravings of a frantic bard.

" SATIRE, whilſt envy and ill-humour ſway

" The mind of man, muſt always make her way;

" Nor to a bofom, with difcretion fraught,

" Is all her malice worth a fingle thought.

" The Wife have not the will, nor Fools the pow'r

" To ſtop her headſtrong courfe ; within the hour,

" Left to herfelf, ſhe dies; oppofing Strife,

" Gives her freſh vigour, and prolongs her life.

" All things her prey, and ev'ry man her aim,

" I can no patent for exemption claim,

" Nor would I wiſh to ſtop that harmlefs dart

" Which plays around, but cannot wound my heart;

" Tho' pointed at myfelf, be SATIRE free ;

" To her 'tis pleafure, and no pain to me."

Diſſembling

Diffembling Wretch! hence to the Stoic fchool,
And there amongft thy breth'ren play the fool,
There, unrebuk'd, thefe wild, vain doctrines preach;
Lives there a man, whom SATIRE cannot reach?
Lives there a man, who calmly can ftand by,
And fee his confcience ripp'd with fteady eye?
When SATIRE flies abroad on Falfhood's wing,
Short is her life, and impotént her fting;
But, when to Truth allied, the wound fhe gives
Sinks deep, and to remoteft ages lives.
When in the tomb thy pamper'd flefh fhall rot,
And e'en by friends thy mem'ry be forgot,
Still fhalt thou live, recorded for thy crimes,
Live in her page, and ftink to after-times.

Haft thou no feeling yet? Come throw off pride,
And own thofe paffions which thou fhalt not hide.
S———, who from the moment of his birth,
Made human nature a reproach on earth,
Who never dar'd, nor wifh'd behind to ftay,
When Folly, Vice, and Meannefs led the way,
Would blufh, fhould he be told, by Truth and Wit,
Thofe actions, which he blufh'd not to commit;

Men

Men the moſt infamous are fond of fame,
And thoſe who fear not guilt, yet ſtart at ſhame.

But whither runs my zeal, whoſe rapid force,
Turning the brain, bears Reaſon from her courſe,
Carries me back to times, when Poets, bleſs'd
With courage, grac'd the Science they profeſs'd;
When they, in Honour rooted, firmly ſtood
The bad to puniſh, and reward the good;
When, to a flame by public Virtue wrought,
The Foes of Freedom they to juſtice brought,
And dar'd expoſe thoſe ſlaves who dar'd ſupport
A Tyrant plan, and call'd themſelves a Court.
Ah! What are Poets now? as ſlaviſh thoſe
Who deal in Verſe, as thoſe who deal in Proſe.
Is there an Author, ſearch the Kingdom round,
In whom true Worth, and real Spirit's found?
The Slaves of Bookſellers, or (doom'd by Fate
To baſer chains) vile penſioners of State;
Some, dead to ſhame, and of thoſe ſhackles proud
Which Honour ſcorns, for ſlav'ry roar aloud,
Others, *half-palſied* only, mutes become,
And what makes SMOLLETT write, makes JOHNSON dumb.

Why

Why turns yon villain pale? why bends his eye
Inward, abaſh'd, when MURPHY paſſes by?
Doſt thou ſage MURPHY for a blockhead take,
Who wages war with Vice for Virtue's ſake?
No, No—like other *Worldlings*, you will find
He ſhifts his ſails, and catches ev'ry wind.
His ſoul the ſhock of int'reſt can't endure:
Give him a penſion then, and ſin ſecure.

With laurell'd wreaths the flatt'rer's brows adorn,
Bid Virtue crouch, bid Vice exalt her horn,
Bid Cowards thrive, put Honeſty to flight,
MURPHY ſhall prove, or try to prove it right.
Try, thou State-Juggler, ev'ry paltry art,
Ranſack the inmoſt cloſet of my heart,
Swear thour't my Friend; by that baſe oath make way
Into my breaſt, and flatter to betray;
Or, if thoſe tricks are vain, if wholeſome doubt
Detects the fraud, and points the Villain out,
Bribe thoſe who daily at my board are fed,
And make them take my life who eat my bread;
On Authors for defence, for praiſe depend;
Pay him but well, and MURPHY is thy friend.

He,

He, he fhall ready ftand with venal rimes,
To varnifh guilt, and confecrate thy crimes,
To make Corruption in falfe colours fhine,
And damn his own good name, to refcue thine.

But, if thy niggard hands their gifts with-hold,
And Vice no longer rains down fhow'rs of gold,
Expect no mercy; facts, well grounded, teach,
MURPHY, if not rewarded, will impeach.
What tho' each man of nice and jufter thought,
Shunning his fteps, decrees, by Honour taught,
He ne'er can be a Friend, who ftoops fo low
To be the bafe betrayer of a foe;
What tho', with thine together link'd, his name
Muft be with thine tranfmitted down to fhame,
To ev'ry manly feeling callous grown,
Rather than not blaft thine, he'll blaft his own.

To ope the fountain, whence fedition fprings,
To flander Government, and libel Kings,
With Freedom's name to ferve a prefent hour,
Tho' born and bred to arbitrary pow'r,
To talk of WILLIAM with infidious art,
Whilft a vile STUART's lurking in his heart,

And,

And, whilft mean Envy rears her loathfome head,
Flatt'ring the living, to abufe the dead,
Where is SHEBBEARE? O, let not foul reproach,
Travelling thither in a City Coach,
The Pill'ry dare to name; the whole intent
Of that Parade was Fame, not Punifhment,
And that old, ftaunch Whig BEARDMORE ftanding by
Can in full Court give that report the lye.

With rude unnat'ral jargon to fupport,
Half *Scotch*, half *Englifh*, a declining Court,
To make moft glaring contraries unite,
And prove, beyond difpute, that black is white,
To make firm Honour tamely league with Shame,
Make Vice and Virtue differ but in name,
To prove that Chains and Freedom are but one,
That to be fav'd muft mean to be undone,
Is there not GUTHRIE? Who, like him, can call
All Oppofites to proof, and conquer all?
He calls forth living waters from the rock;
He calls forth children from the barren ftock;
He, far beyond the fprings of Nature led,
Makes Women bring forth after they are dead;

He,

He, on a curious, new, and happy plan,
In *Wedlock*'s facred bands joins Man to Man ;
And, to complete the whole, moft ftrange, but true,
By fome rare magic, makes them fruitful too,
Whilft from their loins, in the due courfe of years,
Flows the rich blood of GUTHRIE's *Englifh Peers.*

Doft thou contrive fome blacker deed of fhame,
Something which Nature fhudders but to name,
Something which makes the Soul of man retreat,
And the life-blood run backward to her feat ?
Doft thou contrive for fome bafe private end,
Some felfifh view, to hang a trufting friend,
To lure him on, e'en to his parting breath,
And promife life, to work him furer death ?
Grown old in villainy, and dead to grace,
Hell in his heart, and TYBURNE in his face ;
Behold, a Parfon at thy Elbow ftands,
Low'ring damnation, and with open hands
Ripe to betray his Saviour for reward ;
The Atheift Chaplain of an Atheift Lord.

Bred to the Church, and for the gown decreed,
'Ere it was known that I fhould learn to read ;

Tho'

Tho' that was nothing, for my Friends, who knew
What mighty Dullnefs of itfelf could do,
Never defign'd me for a working Prieft,
But hop'd, I fhould have been a DEAN at leaft;
Condemn'd (like many more, and worthier men,
To whom I pledge the fervice of my pen),
Condemn'd (whilft proud, and pamper'd Sons of Lawn,
Cramm'd to the throat, in lazy plenty yawn)
In pomp of *rev'rend begg'ry* to appear,
To pray, and ftarve on forty pounds a year;
My Friends, who never felt the galling load,
Lament that I forfook the Packhorfe road,
Whilft Virtue to my conduct witnefs bears
In throwing off that gown, which FRANCIS wears.

 What Creature's that, fo very pert and prim;
So very full of foppery, and whim;
So gentle, yet fo brifk; fo wond'rous fweet,
So fit to prattle at a Lady's feet,
Who looks, as he the Lord's rich vineyard trod,
And by his Garb appears a man of God?
Truft not to looks, nor credit outward fhow;
The villain lurks beneath the *caffock'd* Beau;

That's

That's an Informer; what avails the name ?
Suffice it that the wretch from SODOM came.

His tongue is deadly—from his prefence run,
Unlefs thy rage would wifh to be undone.
No ties can hold him, no affection bind,
And Fear alone reftrains his coward mind ;
Free him from that, no Monfter is fo fell,
Nor is fo fure a blood-hound found in hell.
His filken fmiles, his hypocritic air,
His meak demeanour, plaufible and fair,
Are only worn to pave Fraud's eafier way,
And make gull'd Virtue fall a furer prey.
Attend his Church—his plan of doctrine view—
The Preacher is a Chriftian, dull, but true ;
But when the hallow'd hour of preaching's o'er,
That plan of doctrine's never thought of more ;
CHRIST is laid by neglected on the fhelf,
And the vile Prieft is Gofpel to himfelf.

By CLELAND tutor'd, and with BLACOW bred,
(BLACOW, whom by a brave refentment led,
OXFORD, if OXFORD had not funk in fame,
Ere this, had damn'd to everlafting fhame)
                                        Their

Their steps he follows, and their crimes partakes,
To Virtue lost, to Vice alone he wakes,
Most lusciously declaims 'gainst luscious themes,
And, whilst he rails at blasphemy, blasphemes.

Are these the Arts, which Policy supplies?
Are these the steps, by which grave Churchmen rise?
Forbid it, Heav'n; or, should it turn out so,
Let me, and mine, continue mean and low.
Such be their Arts, whom Interest controuls;
KIDGELL and I have free and honest souls.
We scorn Preferment which is gain'd by Sin,
And will, tho' poor without, have peace within.

THE

THE

DUELLIST.

THE

UELLIST.

DUELLIST.

BOOK I.

THE Clock ſtruck twelve, o'er half the globe
    Darkneſs had ſpread her pitchy robe;
MORPHEUS, his feet with velvet ſhod,
Treading as if in fear he trod,
Gentle as dews at even-tide,
Diſtill'd his poppies far and wide.

AMBITION, who, when waking, dreams
Of mighty, but phantaftic, fchemes,
Who, when afleep, ne'er knows that reft
With which the humbler foul is bleft,
Was building caftles in the air,
Goodly to look upon and fair,
But, on a bad foundation laid,
Doom'd at return of morn to fade.

Pale STUDY, by the taper's light,
Wearing away the watch of night,
Sat reading, but, with o'ercharg'd head,
Remember'd nothing that he read.

Starving 'midft plenty, with a face
Which might the Court of Famine grace,
Ragged, and filthy to behold,
Grey AV'RICE nodded o'er his gold.

JEALOUSY, his quick eye half-clos'd,
With watchings worn, reluctant doz'd,
And mean diftruft not quite forgot,
Slumber'd as if he flumber'd not.

Stretch'd

Stretch'd at his length on the bare ground,
His hardy offspring sleeping round,
Snor'd *restless* LABOUR ; by his side
Lay HEALTH, a coarse, but comely Bride.

VIRTUE, without the Doctor's aid,
In the soft arms of sleep was laid,
Whilst VICE, within the guilty breast,
Could not be phyfic'd into rest.

Thou Bloody Man! whose ruffian knife
Is drawn against thy neighbour's life,
And never scruples to descend
Into the bosom of a friend,
A firm, fast friend, by vice allied,
And to thy *secret* service tied,
In whom ten Murders breed no awe,
If properly fecur'd from law.
Thou Man of Lust! whom passion fires
To foulest deeds, whose hot desires
O'er honest bars with ease make way,
Whilst *Ideot* Beauty falls a prey,
And to indulge thy brutal flame,
A LUCRECE must be brought to shame,

Who

Who doft, a brave, bold Sinner, bear
Rank inceft to the open air,
And rapes, full-blown upon thy crown,
Enough to weigh a nation down.
Thou Simular of Luft! vain man,
Whofe reftlefs thoughts ftill form the plan
Of guilt, which wither'd to the root,
Thy lifelefs nerves can't execute,
Whilft in thy marrowlefs, dry bones,
Defire without Enjoyment groans.
Thou Perjur'd Wretch! whom Falfhood cloaths
E'n like a garment, who with oaths
Doft trifle, as with brokers, meant
To ferve thy ev'ry vile intent,
In the Day's broad and fearching eye
Making God witnefs to a lye,
Blafpheming Heav'n and Earth for pelf,
And hanging *friends* to fave thyfelf.
Thou Son of Chance! whofe glorious foul
On the four aces doom'd to roll,
Was never yet with Honour caught,
Nor on poor Virtue loft one thought,
Who doft thy *Wife*, thy *Children* fet,
Thy *All*, upon a fingle bet,

Rifquing,

Rifquing, the defp'rate ftake to try,
Here and *Hereafter* on a die,
Who, thy own private fortune loft,
Doft game on at thy Country's coft,
And, grown expert in Sharping rules,
Firft fool'd thyfelf, now prey'ft on fools.
Thou Noble Gamefter, whofe high place
Gives too much credit to difgrace,
Who, with the motion of a die,
Doft make a mighty Ifland fly,
The Sums, I mean, of good *French* gold
For which a mighty Ifland fold;
Who doft *betray Intelligence*,
Abufe the *deareft Confidence*,
And, private fortune to create,
Moft falfely play the game of State;
Who doft within the *Alley* fport
Sums, which might beggar a whole Court,
And make us Bankrupts all, if CARE,
With good *Earl* TALBOT, was not there,
Thou daring Infidel! whom Pride
And Sin have drawn from Reafon's fide,
Who, fearing his avengeful rod,
Doft wifh not to believe a God,

O 3   Whofe

Whose Hope is founded on a plan,
Which should distract the soul of man,
And make him curse his abject birth ;
Whose Hope is, once return'd to earth,
There to lie down, for worms a feast,
To rot and perish, like a Beast ;
Who dost, of punishment afraid,
And by thy crimes a Coward made,
To ev'ry gen'rous soul a Curse,
Than Hell and all her torments worse,
When crawling to thy latter end,
Call on destruction as a friend,
Chusing to crumble into dust
Rather than rise, tho' rise you must.
Thou Hypocrite ! who dost prophane,
And take the Patriot's name in vain,
Then most thy Country's foe, when most
Of Love and Loyalty you boast ;
Who for the filthy love of Gold,
Thy Friend, thy King, thy God hast sold,
And, mocking the just claim of Hell,
Were bidders found, thyself wouldst sell.
Ye Villains ! of whatever name,
Whatever rank, to whom the claim

Of

Of Hell is certain, on whofe lids
That worm, which never dies, forbids
Sweet Sleep to fall, *Come* and *Behold*,
Whilft Envy makes your blood run cold,
Behold, by pitilefs Confcience led,
So JUSTICE wills, that holy bed,
Where PEACE her full dominion keeps,
And Innocence with HOLLAND fleeps.

    Bid Terror, pofting on the wind,
Affray the fpirits of mankind,
Bid Earthquakes, heaving for a vent,
Rive their concealing continent,
And, forcing an untimely birth
Thro' the vaft bowels of the earth,
Endeavour, in her monftrous womb,
At once all Nature to entomb;
Bid all that's horrible and dire,
All that man hates and fears, confpire
To make night hideous, as they can;
Still is thy Sleep, Thou Virtuous Man,
Pure as the Thoughts, which in thy breaft
Inhabit, and enfure thy reft;

Still

Still fhall thy AYLIFF, taught, tho' late,
Thy friendly juftice in his fate,
Turn'd to a guardian Angel, fpread
Sweet dreams of comfort round thy head.

Dark was the Night, by Fate decreed
For the contrivance of a deed
More black than common, which might make
This land from her foundations fhake,
Might tear up Freedom from the root,
Deftroy a WILKES, and fix a BUTE.

Deep Horror held her wide domain ;
The fky in fullen drops of rain
Forewept the morn, and thro' the air,
Which, op'ning, laid its bofom bare,
Loud Thunders roll'd, and Light'ning ftream'd ;
The Owl at Freedom's window fcream'd,
The Screech-Owl, prophet dire, whofe breath
Brings ficknefs, and whofe note is death ;
The Church-Yard teem'd, and from the tomb,
All fad and filent, thro' the gloom,
The Ghofts of Men, in former times
Whofe Public Virtues were their crimes,

Indignant

Indignant ſtalk'd; Sorrow and Rage
Blank'd their pale cheek; in his own age
The prop of Freedom, HAMPDEN there
Felt after death the gen'rous care;
SIDNEY by grief from Heav'n was kept,
And for his brother Patriot wept;
All Friends of LIBERTY, when Fate
Prepar'd to ſhorten WILKES's date,
Heav'd, deeply hurt, the heart-felt groan,
And knew that wound to be their own.

Hail, LIBERTY! a glorious word,
In other countries ſcarcely heard,
Or heard but as a thing of courſe,
Without or Energy or Force;
Here felt, enjoy'd, ador'd ſhe ſprings,
Far, far beyond the reach of Kings,
Freſh blooming from our Mother Earth;
With Pride and Joy ſhe owns her birth
Deriv'd from us, and in return
Bids in our breaſts her Genius burn;
Bids us with all thoſe bleſſings live
Which LIBERTY alone can give,

Or

Or nobly with that Spirit die,
Which makes Death more than Victory.

Hail thofe Old Patriots, on whofe tongue
Perfuafion in the Senate hung,
Whilft They the facred Caufe maintain'd!
Hail thofe Old Chiefs, to Honour train'd,
Who fpread, when other methods fail'd,
War's bloody banner, and prevail'd!
Shall Men like thefe unmention'd fleep
Promifcuous with the common heap,
And (Gratitude forbid the crime)
Be carried down the ftream of Time
In Shoals, unnotic'd and forgot,
On LETHE's ftream, like flags, to rot?
No—they fhall live, and each fair name,
Recorded in the book of Fame,
Founded on Honour's bafis, faft
As the round Earth to ages laft.
Some Virtues vanifh with our breath,
Virtue like this lives after death.
Old Time himfelf, his fcythe thrown by,
Himfelf loft in Eternity,

An

An everlasting crown shall twine
To make a WILKES and SIDNEY join.

But should some slave-got Villain dare
Chains for his Country to prepare,
And, by his birth to slav'ry broke,
Make her to feel the galling yoke,
May he be evermore accurs'd,
Amongst bad men be rank'd the worst ;
May he be still himself, and still
Go on in Vice, and perfect Ill ;
May his broad crimes each day increase,
'Till he can't Live, nor Die in Peace ;
May he be plung'd so deep in shame
That Satan mayn't endure his name,
And hear, scarce crawling on the earth,
His children curse him for their birth ;
May LIBERTY, beyond the grave,
Ordain him to be still a slave,
Grant him what here he most requires,
And damn him with his own desires !

But should some Villain, in support
And zeal for a despairing Court,

Placing

Placing in Craft his confidence,

And making Honour a pretence

To do a deed of deepeft fhame,

Whilft filthy lucre is his aim ;

Should fuch a Wretch, with fword or knife,

Contrive to practife 'gainft the life

Of One, who honour'd thro' the land,

'For Freedom made a glorious ftand,

Whofe chief, perhaps his only crime,

Is (if plain Truth at fuch a time

May dare her fentiments to tell)

That He his Country loves too well ;

May He—but words are all too weak

The feelings of my heart to fpeak—

May He—O for a noble curfe

Which might his very marrow pierce—

The general contempt engage,

And be the MARTIN of his age.

END of the FIRST BOOK.

THE

T H E

D U E L L I S T.

B O O K   II.

D EEP in the bosom of a wood,
    Out of the road, a Temple stood;
Antient, and much the worse for wear,
It call'd aloud for quick repair,
And, tottering from side to side,
Menac'd destruction far and wide,
Nor able seem'd, unless made stronger,
To hold out four or five years longer.
Four hundred pillars, from the ground.
Rising in order, *most* unsound,

Some

Some rotten to the heart aloof
Seem'd to fupport the tott'ring roof,
But to infpection nearer laid,
Inftead of giving wanted aid.

The Structure, rare and curious, made
By Men moft famous in their trade,
A work of years, admir'd by all,
Was fuffer'd into duft to fall,
Or, juft to mak it hang together,
And keep off the effects of weather,
Was patch'd and patch'd from time to time
By wretches, whom it were a crime
A crime, which Art would treafon hold,
To mention with thofe names of old.

Builders, who had the pile furvey'd,
And thofe not *Flitcrofts* in their trade,
Doubted (the wife hand in a doubt
Merely fometimes to hand her out)
Whether (like Churches in a brief,
Taught wifely to obtain relief
Thro' Chancery, who gives her fees
To this and other Charities)

It muſt not, in all parts unſound,
Be ripp'd, and pull'd down to the ground;
Whether (tho' after-ages ne'er
Shall raiſe a building to compare)
Art, if they ſhould their Art employ,
Meant to preſerve, might not deſtroy.
As human bodies, worn away,
Batter'd and haſting to decay,
Bidding the pow'r of Art deſpair,
Cannot thoſe very medicines bear,
Which, and which only can reſtore,
And make them healthy as before.

　To LIBERTY, whoſe gracious ſmile
Shed peace and plenty o'er the Iſle,
Our grateful Anceſtors, her plain
But faithful Children, rais'd this ſane.

　Full in the Front, ſtretch'd out in length,
Where Nature put forth all her ſtrength
In Spring eternal, lay a plain,
Where our brave fathers us'd to train
Their Sons to Arms, to teach the Art
Of War, and ſteel the infant heart.

LABOUR,

LABOUR, their hardy nurſe, when young,
Their joints had knit, their nerves had ſtrung;
ABSTINENCE, foe declar'd to death,
Had, from the time they firſt drew breath,
The beſt of doctors, with plain food,
Kept pure the channel of their blood;
HEALTH in their checks bade colour riſe,
And GLORY ſparkled in their eyes.

The inſtruments of Huſbandry,
As in contempt, were all thrown by,
And, flattering a manly pride,
War's keener tools their place ſupplied.
Their arrows to the head they drew;
Swift to the point their javelins flew;
They graſp'd the ſword, they ſhook the ſpear;
Their Fathers felt a pleaſing fear,
And even COURAGE, ſtanding by,
Scarcely beheld with ſteady eye.
Each Stripling, leſſon'd by his Sire,
Knew when to cloſe, when to retire,
When near at hand, when from afar
To fight, and was Himſelf a War.

Their

Their Wives, their Mothers all around,
Carelefs of order, on the ground,
Breath'd forth to Heav'n the pious vow,
And for a Son's or Hufband's brow,
With eager fingers Laurel wove;
Laurel, which in the facred grove,
Planted by LIBERTY, they find,
The brows of Conquerors to bind,
To give them Pride and Spirits, fit
To make a world in arms fubmit.

What raptures did the bofom fire
Of the young, rugged, peafant Sire,
When, from the toil of mimic fight,
Returning with return of Night,
He faw his babe refign the breaft,
And, fmiling, ftroke thofe arms in jeft,
With which hereafter he fhall make
The proudeft heart in GALLIA quake!

Gods! with what joy, what honeft pride,
Did each fond, wifhing, ruftic Bride,
Behold her manly fwain return!
How did her love-fick bofom burn,

Tho' on Parades he was not bred,
Nor wore the livery of red,
When, Pleasure height'ning all her charms,
She strain'd her Warrior in her arms,
And begg'd, whilst Love and Glory fire,
A Son, a Son just like his Sire!

Such were the men in former times,
Ere Luxury had made our crimes
Our bitter Punishment, who bore
Their terrors to a foreign shore;
Such were the men, who free from dread,
By EDWARDS and by HENRIES led,
Spread, like a torrent swell'd with rains,
O'er haughty GALLIA's trembling plains;
Such were the Men, when lust of Pow'r,
To work him woe, in evil hour
Debauch'd the Tyrant from those ways,
On which a King should found his praise,
When stern OPPRESSION, hand in hand
With PRIDE, stalk'd proudly thro' the land;
When weeping JUSTICE was misled
From her fair course, and MERCY dead;

Such

Such were the Men, in Virtue ſtrong,
Who dar'd not ſee their Country's wrong,
Who left the mattock, and the ſpade,
And, in the robes of War array'd,
In their rough arms, departing, took
Their helpleſs babes, and with a look
Stern and determin'd, ſwore to ſee
Thoſe babes no more, or ſee them free;
Such were the Men whom Tyrant PRIDE
Could never faſten to his ſide
By threats or bribes, who, Freemen born,
Chains, tho' of gold, beheld with ſcorn;
Who, free from ev'ry ſervile awe,
Could never be divorc'd from Law,
From that broad gen'ral Law, which Senſe
Made for the general defence;
Could never yield to partial ties
Which from dependant ſtations riſe;
Could never be to Slav'ry led,
For PROPERTY was at their head;
Such were the Men in days of yore,
Who, call'd by LIBERTY, before
Her Temple on the ſacred green,
In martial paſtimes oft were ſeen—

Now

Now feen no longer—in their ftead,
To lazinefs and vermin bred,
A Race who, ftrangers to the caufe
Of Freedom, live by other laws,
On other motives fight, a prey
To intereft, and flaves for pay.
VALOUR, how glorious on a plan
Of Honour founded, leads their Van;
DISCRETION, free from taint of fear,
Cool, but refolv'd, brings up their rear,
DISCRETION, VALOUR's better half;
DEPENDANCE holds the Gen'ral's Staff.

In plain and home-fpun garb array'd,
Not for vain fhew, but fervice made,
In a green flourifhing old age,
Not damn'd yet with an Equipage,
In rules of *Porterage* untaught,
SIMPLICITY, not worth a groat,
For years had kept the Temple door;
Full on his breaft a glafs he wore,
Thro' which his bofom open lay
To ev'ry one that pafs'd that way.

Now

Now turn'd adrift—with humbler face,
But prouder heart, his vacant place
CORRUPTION fills, and bears the key;
No entrance now without a fee.

With belly round, and full fat face,
Which on the houſe reflected grace,
Full of good fare, and honeſt glee,
The *Steward* HOSPITALITY,
Old WELCOME ſmiling by his ſide,
A good, old Servant, often tried,
And faithful found, who kept in view
His Lady's fame and int'reſt too,
Who made each heart with joy rebound,
Yet never run her State a-ground,
Was turn'd off, or (which word I find
Is more in modern uſe) *reſign'd.*

Half-ſtarv'd, half-ſtarving others, bred
In beggary, with carrion fed,
Deteſted, and deteſting all,
Made up of Avarice and Gall,
Boaſting great thrift, yet waſting more
Than ever Steward did before,

P 3

Succeeded

Succeeded *One*, who, to engage
The praife of an exhaufted Age,
Affum'd a name of high degree,
And call'd himfelf OECONOMY.

Within the Temple, full in fight,
Where, without ceafing, day and night,
The Workmen toil'd, where LABOUR bar'd
His brawny arm, where ART prepar'd,
In regular and even rows,
Her types, a *Printing-Prefs* arofe ;
Each Workman knew his tafk, and each
Was honeft and expert as LEACH.

Hence LEARNING ftruck a deeper root,
And SCIENCE brought forth riper fruit ;
Hence LOYALTY receiv'd fupport,
Even when banifh'd from the Court ;
Hence GOVERNMENT gain'd ftrength, and *hence*
RELIGION fought, and found defence ;
. *Hence* ENGLAND's faireft fame arofe,
And LIBERTY fubdu'd her foes.

On

On a low, fimple, turf-made throne
Rais'd by *Allegiance*, fcarcely known
From her attendants, glad to be
Pattern of that Equality
She wifh'd to all, fo far as cou'd
Safely confift with focial good,
The GODDESS fat; around her head
A chearful radiance GLORY fpread;
COURAGE, a Youth of royal race,
Lovelily ftern, poffefs'd a place
On her left-hand, and on her right
Sat HONOUR, cloath'd with robes of Light;
Before her MAGNA CHARTA lay,
Which fome great Lawyer, of his day
The PRATT, was offic'd to explain,
And make the bafis of her reign;
PEACE, crown'd with Olive, to her breaft
Two fmiling, twin-born infants preft;
At her feet couching, WAR was laid,
And with a brindled Lion play'd;
JUSTICE and MERCY, hand in hand,
Joint Guardians of the happy land,
Together held their mighty charg·,
And TRUTH walk'd all about at large;

HEALTH

HEALTH for the royal troop the feaft
Prepar'd, and VIRTUE was High Prieft.

Such was the fame our *Goddefs* bore,
Her Temple fuch, in days of yote.
What changes ruthlefs Time prefents !
Behold her ruin'd battlements,
Her walls decay'd, her nodding fpires,
Her altars broke, her dying fires,
Her name defpis'd, her Priefts deftroy'd,
Her friends difgrac'd, her foes employ'd,
Herfelf (by *Minifterial* Arts
Depriv'd e'en of the people's hearts,
Whilft They, to work her furer woe,
Feign her to Monarchy a foe)
Exil'd by grief, felf-doom'd to dwell
With fome poor Hermit in a cell,
Or, that retirement tedious grown,
If fhe walks forth, fhe walks *unknown*,
Hooted, and pointed at with fcorn,
As One in fome ftrange Country born.

Behold a rude and ruffian race,
A band of fpoilers, feize her place;

With

With looks, which might the heart dif-feat,
And make life found a quick retreat,
To rapine from the cradle bred,
A *Staunch, Old Blood-hound* at their head,
Who, free from Virtue and from Awe,
Knew none but the bad part of Law;
They rov'd at large ; each on his breaft
Mark'd with a *Grey-hound,* ftood confeft.
CONTROULMENT waited on their nod
High-weilding PERSECUTION's rod,
CONFUSION follow'd at their heels,
And a *caft Statefman* held the Seals,
Thofe Seals, for which he dear fhall pay,
When awful JUSTICE takes her day.

 The Printers faw—they faw and fled—
SCIENCE, declining, hung her head,
PROPERTY in defpair appear'd,
And for herfelf deftruction fear'd ;
Whilft, under-foot, the rude flaves trod
The works of men, and word of God,
Whilft, clofe behind, on many a book,
In which he never deigns to look,

         Which

Which he did not, nay—could not read,
A *bold*, *bad* man (by pow'r decreed
For that bad end, who in the dark
Scorn'd to do mifchief) fet his mark
In the full day, the mark of Hell,
And on the Gofpel ftamp'd an L.

LIBERTY fled, her Friends withdrew,
Her Friends, a faithful, chofen few ;
HONOUR in grief threw up, and SHAME,
Cloathing herfelf with HONOUR's name,
Ufurp'd his ftation ; on the throne,
Which LIBERTY once call'd her own,
(Gods, that fuch mighty ills fhould fpring,
Under fo great, fo good a King,
So Lov'd, fo Loving, thro' the arts
Of Statefmen, curs'd with wicked hearts!)
For ev'ry darker purpofe fit,
Behold in triumph STATE-CRAFT fit.

END OF THE SECOND BOOK.

THE

DUELLIST.

BOOK III.

AH me! what mighty perils wait,
The man who meddles with a State,
Whether to ftrengthen, or oppofe!
Falfe are his friends, and firm his foes.
How muft his Soul, once ventur'd in,
Plunge blindly on from fin to fin!
What toils he fuffers, what difgrace,
To get, and then to keep a place!
How often, whether wrong or right,
Muft he in jeft or earneft fight,
Rifquing for thofe both life and limb,
Who would not rifque one groat for him!

Under

Under the Temple lay a Cave;
Made by fome guilty, coward flave,
Whofe actions fear'd rebuke, a maze
Of intricate and winding ways,
Not to be found without a clue;
One Paffage only, known to few,
In paths direct led to a Cell,
Where FRAUD in fecret lov'd to dwell,
With all her tools and flaves about her,
Nor fear'd left HONESTY fhould rout her.

In a dark corner, fhunning fight
Of Man, and fhrinking from the light,
One dull, dim taper thro' the Cell
Glimm'ring, to make more horrible
The face of darknefs, fhe prepares,
Working unfeen, all kinds of fnares,
With curious, but deftructive art;
Here, thro' the eye to catch the heart,
Gay *Stars* their tinfel beams afford,
Neat artifice to trap a Lord;
There, fit for all whom Folly bred,
Wave *Plumes* of *Feathers* for the head;

Garters

Garters the Hag contrives to make,
Which, as it feems, a babe might break;
But which ambitious Madmen feel
More firm and fure than chains of fteel;
Which, flipp'd juft underneath the knee,
Forbid a Freeman to be free.
Purfes fhe knew (did ever curfe
Travel more fure than in a purfe?)
Which, by fome ftrange and magic bands
Enflave the foul, and tie the hands.

   Here FLATT'RY, eldeft born of GUILE,
Weaves with rare fkill the filken fmile,
The courtly cringe, the fupple bow,
The private fqueeze, the Levee vow,
With which, no ftrange or recent cafe,
Fools *in* deceive Fools *out* of place.

   CORRUPTION (who, in former times,
Thro' fear or fhame conceal'd her crimes,
And what fhe did, contriv'd to do it
So that the Public might not view it)
Prefumptuous grown, unfit was held
For their dark councils, and expell'd,

                          Since

Since in the day her bufinefs might
Be done as fafe as in the night.

Her eye down-bending to the ground,
Planning fome dark and deadly wound,
Holding a dagger, on which ftood,
All frefh and reeking, drops of blood,
Bearing a lanthorn, which of yore,
By TREASON borrow'd, GUY FAWKES bore,
By which, fince they improv'd in trade,
Excifemen have their lanthorns made,
ASSASSINATION, her whole mind,
Blood-thirfting, on her arm reclin'd.
DEATH, grinning, at her elbow ftood,
And held forth inftruments of blood,
Vile inftruments, which cowards chufe,
But Men of Honour dare not ufe ;
Around his Lordfhip and his Grace,
Both qualified for fuch a place,
With many a FORBES, and many a DUN,
Each a refolv'd, and pious Son,
Wait her high bidding; Each prepar'd
As fhe around her orders fhar'd,

Proof

Proof 'gainſt remorſe, to run, to fly,
And bid the deſtin'd victim die,
Poſting on Villainy's black wing,
Whether He Patriot is, or King.

Oppreſſion, willing to appear
An object of our love, not fear,
Or at the moſt a rev'rend awe
To breed, uſurp'd the garb of Law.
A Book ſhe held, on which her eyes
Were deeply fix'd, whence ſeem'd to riſe
Joy in her breaſt ; a Book, of might
Moſt wonderful, which black to white
Could turn, and without help of laws,
Could make the worſe the better cauſe.
She read, by flatt'ring hopes deceiv'd,
She wiſh'd, and what ſhe wiſh'd, believ'd,
To make that Book for ever ſtand
The rule of wrong through all the land ;
On the back, fair and worthy note,
At large was Magna Charta wrote,
But turn your eye within, and read,
A bitter leſſon, N——'s Creed.

Ready,

Ready, e'en with a look, to run,
Faſt as the courſers of the Sun,
To worry Virtue; at her hand
Two half-ſtarv'd Greyhounds took their ſtand.
A curious model, cut in wood,
Of a moſt antient Caſtle ſtood,
Full in her view; the gates were barr'd,
And Soldiers on the watch kept guard;
In the front, openly, in black
Was wrote, The Tow'r, but on the back,
Mark'd with a Secretary's ſeal,
In bloody Letters, The Baſtile.

Around a Table, fully bent
On miſchief of moſt black intent
Deeply determin'd, that their reign
Might longer laſt, to work the bane
Of one firm Patriot, whoſe heart, tied
To Honour, all their pow'r defied,
And brought thoſe actions into light
They wiſh'd to have conceal'd in Night.
Begot, Born, Bred to infamy,
A Privy-Council ſat of Three;

Great were their names, of high repute
And favour thro' the land of BUTE.

The FIRST (entitled to the place
Of Honour both by Gown and Grace,
Who never let occasion slip
To take right hand of fellowship,
And was so proud, that should he meet
The twelve Apostles in the street,
He'd turn his nose up at them all,
And shove his Saviour from the wall;
Who was so mean (Meanness and Pride
Still go together side by side)
That he would cringe, and creep, be civil,
And hold a stirrup for the Devil,
If in a journey to his mind,
He'd let him mount, and ride behind;
Who basely fawn'd thro' all his life,
For *Patrons* first, then for a *Wife*.
Wrote *Dedications* which must make
The heart of ev'ry Christian quake;
Made one Man equal to, or more
Than God, then left him, as before

His God he left, and drawn by Pride,
Shifted about to t'other fide)
Was by his fire a Parfon m de,
Merely to give the Boy a trade;
But he himfelf was thereto drawn
By fome faint omens of the Lawn,
And on the truly Chriftian plan
To make himfelf a Gentleman,
A title, in which form array'd him,
Tho' Fate ne'er thought on't when fhe made him.

The Oaths he took, 'tis very true,
But took them, as all wife men do,
With an intent, if things fhould turn,
Rather to temporize, than burn.
Gofpel and Loyalty were made
To ferve the purpofes of trade;
Religion's are but paper ties,
Which bind the fool, but which the wife,
Such idle notions far above,
Draw on and off, juft like a glove;
All Gods, all Kings (let his great aim
Be anfwer'd) were to him the fame.

A Curate firſt, he read and read,
And laid in, whilſt he ſhould have fed
The ſouls of his neglected flock,
Of reading ſuch a mighty ſtock,
That he o'ercharg'd the weary brain
With more than ſhe could well contain,
More than ſhe was with Spirits fraught
To turn, and methodize to Thought,
And which, like ill-digeſted food,
To humours turn'd, and not to blood.
Brought up to London, from the plow
And Pulpit, how to make a bow
He try'd to learn, he grew polite,
And was the Poet's Paraſite.
With Wits converſing (and Wits then
Were to be found 'mongſt Noblemen)
He caught, or would have caught the flame,
And would be nothing, or the ſame;
He drank with Drunkards, liv'd with Sinners,
Herded with Infidels for dinners,
With ſuch an Emphaſis and Grace
Blaſphem'd, that POTTER kept not pace;
He, in the higheſt reign of noon,
Bawl'd bawdry ſongs to a Pſalm Tune,

Liv'd

Liv'd with Men infamous and vile,
Truck'd his falvation for a fmile,
To catch their humour caught their plan,
And laugh'd at God to laugh with Man,
Prais'd them, when living, in each breath,
And damn'd their mem'ries after death.

To prove his Faith, which all admit
Is at leaft equal to his Wit,
And make himfelf a Man of note,
He in defence of Scripture wrote ;
So long he wrote, and long about it,
That e'en Believers 'gan to doubt it ;
He wrote too of the Inward Light,
Tho' no one knew how he came by't,
And of that influencing Grace,
Which in his life ne'er found a place ;
He wrote too of the Holy Ghoft,
Of whom, no more than doth a poft
He knew, nor, fhould an Angel fhew him,
Would He or know, or chufe to know him.

Next (for he knew 'twixt ev'ry Science
There was a natural alliance)

He

He wrote, t' advance his Maker's praife,
Comments on rimes, and notes on plays,
And with an all-fufficient air
Plac'd himfelf in the Critic's chair,
Ufurp'd o'er Reafon full dominion,
And govern'd merely by opinion.
At length dethron'd, and kept in awe
By one plain fimple Man of Law,
He arm'd dead Friends, to Vengeance true,
T' abufe the Man they never knew.

Examine ftrictly all mankind,
Moft Characters are mix'd we find,
And Vice and Virtue take their turn
In the fame breaft to beat and burn.
Our Prieft was an exception here,
Nor did one fpark of Grace appear,
Not one dull, dim fpark in his foul ;
Vice, glorious Vice poffefs'd the whole,
And, in her fervice truly warm,
He was in fin moft uniform.

Injurious *Satire*, own at leaft
One fniveling Virtue in the Prieft,

One

One fniveling Virtue which is plac'd,
They fay, in or about the waift,
Call'd CHASTITY ; the Prudifh Dame
Knows it at large by Virtue's name.
To this his Wife (and in thefe days
Wives feldom without reafon praife)
Tears evidence—then calls her child,
And fwears that TOM was vaftly wild.

    Ripen'd by a long courfe of years,
He great and perfect now appears.
In fhape fcarce of the human kind ;
A Man, without a manly mind ;
No hufband, tho' he's truly wed ;
Tho' on his knees a child is bred,
No Father ; injur'd, without end
A Foe ; and, tho' oblig'd, no Friend ;
A Heart, which Virtue ne'er difgrac'd ;
A Head, where Learning runs to wafte ;
A Gentleman well-bred, if breeding
Refts in the article of reading ;   ·
A Man of this World, for the next
Was ne'er included in his text ;

A

A Judge of Genius, tho' confeſt
With not one ſpark of Genius bleſt ;
Amongſt the firſt of Critics plac'd,
Tho' free from ev'ry taint of Taſte ;
A Chriſtian without faith or works,
As he would be a Turk 'mongſt Turks ;
A great Divine, as Lords agree,
Without the leaſt Divinity ;
To crown all, in declining age,
Enflam'd with Church and Party-rage,
Behold him, full and perfect quite,
A falſe Saint, and true Hypocrite.

Next ſat a *Lawyer*, often try'd
In perilous extremes ; when Pride
And Pow'r, all wild and trembling, ſtood,
Nor dar'd to tempt the raging flood ;
This bold, bad Man aroſe to view,
And gave his hand to help them through,
Steel'd 'gainſt Compaſſion, as they paſt,
He ſaw poor Freedom breathe her laſt,
He ſaw her ſtruggle, heard her groan,
He ſaw her helpleſs and alone,

Q 4   Whelm'd

Whelm'd in that ſtorm, which, fear'd and prais'd
By ſlaves leſs bold, himſelf had rais'd,

Bred to the Law, he from the firſt
Of all bad Lawyers was the wcrſt.
Perfection (for bad men maintain
In ill we may perfection gain)
In others is a work of time,
And they creep on from crime to crime,
He, for a Prodigy deſign'd
To ſpread amazement o'er mankind,
Started full ripen'd all at once
A Perfect Knave, and Perfect Dunce.

Who will for him may boaſt of Senſe,
His better guard is Impudence.
His front, with ten-fold plates of braſs
Secur'd, SHAME never yet could paſs,
Nor on the ſurface of his ſkin,
Bluſh for that guilt which dwelt within.
How often, in contempt of Laws,
To found the bottom of a cauſe,
To ſearch out ev'ry rotten part,
And worm into its very heart,

Hath

Hath he ta'en briefs on falfe pretence,
And undertaken the defence
Of trufting Fools, whom in the end
He meant to ruin, not defend?
How often, e'en in open Court,
Hath the wretch made his fhame his fport,
And laugh'd off, with a Villain's eafe,
Throwing up briefs, and keeping fees?
Such things, as, tho' to roguery bred,
Had ftruck a little Villain dead.

Caufes, whatever their import,
He undertakes, to ferve a Court;
For he by heart this rule had got,
Pow'r can effect, what Law cannot.

Fools he forgives, but rogues he fears;
If Genius, yok'd with Worth, appears,
His weak foul fickens at the fight,
And ftrives to plunge them down in night.

So loud he talks, fo very loud,
He is an Angel with the crowd,
Whilft he makes Juftice hang her head,
And Judges turn from pale to red.   Bid

Bid all that Nature, on a plan
Moft intimate, makes dear to Man,
All that with grand and gen'ral ties
Binds good and bad, the Fool and Wife,
Knock at his Heart ; They knock in vain,
No entrance there fuch Suitors gain.
Bid kneeling Kings forfake the throne ;
Bid at his feet his Country groan;
Bid Liberty ftretch out her hands ;
Rel'gion plead her ftronger bands ;
Bid Parents, Children, Wife, and Friends ;
If they come thwart his private ends,
Unmov'd he hears the gen'ral call,
And bravely tramples on them all.

Who will, for him, may cant and whine,
And let weak Confcience with her line
Chalk out their ways ; fuch ftarving rules
Are only fit for coward fools,
Fellows who credit what Priefts tell,
And tremble at the thoughts of Hell ;
His Spirit dares contend with Grace,
And meets Damnation face to face.

Such

Such was our *Lawyer*; by his fide
In all bad qualities allied,
In all bad Counfels, fat a *Third*,
By birth a Lord; O facred word!
O word moft facred, whence Men get
A Priviledge to run in debt,
Whence They at large exemption claim
From Satire, and her fervant Shame;
Whence They, depriv'd of all her force,
Forbid bold Truth to hold her courfe.

Confult his perfon, drefs, and air,
He feems, which ftrangers well might fwear,
The Mafter, or by *Courtefy*,
The Captain of a Colliery.
Look at his vifage, and agree
Half-Hang'd he feems, juft from the Tree
Efcap'd; a Rope may fometimes break,
Or Men be cut down by miftake.

He hath not Virtue, (in the fchool
Of Vice bred up) to live by rule,
Nor hath he Senfe (which none can doubt
Who know the Man) to live without.

His life is a continu'd scene
Of all that's infamous and mean;
He knows not change, unless, grown nice
And delicate, from vice to vice;
Nature, design'd him, in a rage,
To be the WHARTON of his age,
But, having giv'n all the Sin,
Forgot to put the Virtues in.
To run a horse, to make a match,
To revel deep, to roar a catch,
To knock a tott'ring watchman down,
To sweat a woman of the Town,
By fits to keep the Peace, or break it,
In turn to give a Pox, or take it,
He is, in faith, most excellent,
And in the Word's most full intent,
A true Choice Spirit we admit;
With Wits a Fool, with Fools a Wit;
Hear him but talk, and You would swear
OBSCENITY herself was there;
And that PROPHANENESS had made choice,
By way of Trump, to use his Voice;
That, in all mean and low things great,
He had been bred at *Billingsgate*,

                                    And

And that, afcending to the earth
Before the feafon of his birth,
BLASPHEMY, making way and room,
Had mark'd him in his Mother's womb;
Too honeft (for the worft of men
In forms are honeft now and then)
Not to have, in the ufual way,
His Bills fent in; Too great, to pay;
Too proud to fpeak to, if he meets,
The honeft Tradefman whom he cheats;
Too infamous to have a friend,
Too bad for bad men to commend,
Or Good to name; beneath whofe weight
Earth groans; who hath been fpar'd by Fate
Only to fhew, on Mercy's plan,
How far and long God bears with Man.

Such were the THREE, who, mocking fleep,
At Midnight fat, in Counfel deep,
Plotting deftruction 'gainft a head,
Whofe Wifdom could not be mifled;
Plotting deftruction 'gainft a heart,
Which ne'er from honour would depart.

. " Is

" Is He not rank'd amongſt our foes ?

" Hath not his Spirit dar'd oppoſe

" Our deareſt meaſures, made our name

" Stand forward on the roll of Shame ?

" Hath he not won the vulgar tribes,

" By ſcorning menaces and bribes,

" And proving, that'his darling cauſe,

" Is of their Liberties ánd Laws

" To ſtand the Champion ? in a word,

" Nor need one argument be heard

" Beyond this, to awake our zeal,

" To quicken our reſolves, and ſteel

" Our ſteady ſouls to bloody bent,

" (Sure ruin to each dear intent,

" Each flatt'ring hope) He, without fear,

" Hath dar'd to make the *Truth* appear."

 They ſaid, and, by reſentment taught,

Each on revenge employ'd his thought,

Each, bent on miſchief, rack'd his brain

To her full ſtretch, but rack'd in vain ;

Scheme after Scheme they brought to view ;

All were examined, none would do.

                                   When

When FRAUD, with pleasure in her face,
Forth issued from her hiding place,
And at the table where they meet,
First having blest them, took her seat.
" No trifling cause, my darling Boys,
" Your present thoughts and cares employs;
" No common snare, no random blow
" Can work the bane of such a Foe,
" By Nature cautious as he's brave,
" To *Honour* only he's a slave;
" In that weak part without defence,
" We must to *Honour* make pretence;
" That Lure shall to his ruin draw
" The Wretch, who stands secure in Law.
" Nor think that I have idly plann'd
" This full-ripe scheme; behold at hand,
" With three months training on his head,
" An Instrument, whom I have bred,
" Born of these bowels, far from sight
" Of Virtue's false, but glaring Light,
" My youngest Born, my dearest Joy,
" Most like myself, my darling Boy.
" He, never touch'd with vile remorse,
" Resolv'd and crafty in his course,

" Shall

" Shall work our ends, complete our fchemes,

" Moft *Mine*, when moft he *Honour*'s feems ;

" Nor can be found, at home, abroad,

" So firm and full a flave of FRAUD."

She faid, and from each envious Son

A difcontented murmur run

Around the Table ; All in place

Thought his full praife their own difgrace,

Wond'ring what Stranger She had got,

Who had one vice that they had not.

When ftrait the portals open flew,

And, clad in armour, to their view

M——, the *Duellift*, came forth ;

All knew, and all confeft his worth,

All juftified, with fmiles array'd,

The happy choice their Dam had made.

END OF THE DUELLIST;

AND

THE SECOND VOLUME.

www.ingramcontent.com/pod-product-compliance
Lightning Source LLC
Chambersburg PA
CBHW030819020726
47499CB00006B/1987